ONCE UPON A DUKE

ERICA RIDLEY

ISBN: 1943794529
ISBN-13: 978-1943794522
Copyright © 2018 Erica Ridley
Model Photography © PeriodImages
Cover Design © Teresa Spreckelmeyer

*W*inter enveloped the frost-tipped forest in its deathly grip as a lone black carriage made its determined way up the side of the frozen mountain.

Benjamin Ward, the fifth Duke of Silkridge, glowered at the sleet obstructing the view from the window. Instead of being ensconced in the dry warmth of his familiar study in London, he was almost four hundred miles north, heading back to the one place he had vowed never to return.

Cressmouth, England.

The nearer his coach drew to the tiny village nestled on the mountain, the worse the weather became. The cold breeze had turned into a punishing wind, and the endless gray skies above had begun to clot with heavy clouds.

Already, blobs too icy to be rain and too wet to be snow spit down upon him.

Bad weather was a good sign. It meant he was getting closer to his goal. Closer to the end. The sooner he fetched the heirloom that had been stolen from him, the sooner he could return to London. Back to where he belonged.

Benjamin clenched his jaw and tore his gaze from the countryside. He hated to leave his home. This was the first time he'd been called away in years. The first time he'd allowed a deviation from his rigid timetable.

Whether Parliament was in session or not, there was too much work to be done back home. Benjamin was personally responsible for half a dozen committees shaping the country's future. He had no time for distracting quests.

But here he was.

His horses clomped past a large, festive sign held sturdy in the frozen ground by thick wooden posts. Despite the darkening sky and the falling sleet, its boldly lettered words were still legible.

Welcome to Christmas!

"It's *Cressmouth*, not Christmas," he muttered beneath his breath.

But it was no use. The quaint northern village was even worse than he remembered. Brightly colored cottages dotted amongst the white of the snow and the frosted tips of a thousand evergreens.

Everywhere he looked there were sparkling candelabra in windowpanes, curling smoke rising merrily from red brick chimneys, children in colorful woolen mittens pelting each other with soft balls of snow.

"Humbug," he muttered. *He* would not take part.

But it was too late. The Silkridge ducal crest gracing the sides of his stately coach had caught the attention of those he passed.

"Ho, there," called out a ruddy-cheeked gentleman shoveling snow from his walk. "Happy Christmas!"

"It's January," Benjamin muttered to his valet.

"Didn't you see the sign?" Doyle answered with a grin. "'Tis always Christmastide here."

"Humbug," the duke said and motioned the driver onward.

The only explanation for the inhabitants' Christmas fervor was their sad and desperate attempt to try to create some sort of advantage to living in the coldest corner of all of England.

Benjamin glared at the snow-dusted pines dipping and curving down the mountain. Cressmouth was in the middle of nowhere. The closest town was Cornhill-on-Tweed. Any further north, and this village would be in Scotland.

A bright red ball sailed from between a pair of cottages and out into the street.

The horses reared in alarm. The driver struggled to keep control of the reins.

From the corner of Benjamin's eye, he caught a flash of movement. A lad scarcely six years of age intended to dart out before the horses in order to retrieve his ball.

"*Stay*," the duke barked, not to his horses and driver, but to the child at the edge of the street.

He leapt from the coach and hurled the ball far over the child's head so that he would be forced to run away from the lane to fetch it.

"So kind of you," called a woman from an open doorway. "You saved Nigel's life."

Benjamin might not love the festive season, but he liked children. They did not deserve ill fates. He gave a stiff nod to the woman and jumped back into the carriage.

His shoulders tightened. He was tired of the cold, tired of traveling, tired of waiting this long to regain something he had lost.

Not Christmas. He had given that up on purpose. Benjamin was after something far more precious.

At tomorrow morning's reading of the will, his mother's heirloom would return where it belonged. To Benjamin's hands. Finally.

The dizzying white castle seemed to mock him from the peak of the mountain. That had been his maternal grandfather's home. His *estranged* grandfather. The same grandfather responsible for reviving what had once been a ghostly settlement into a vibrant Christmas village.

A madman. There was no other explanation.

Benjamin directed his driver toward the winding path up to the castle's imposing portcullis. They would sleep here tonight. There were no other inns. Besides, this had once been his winter home.

Although his paternal grandfather had passed

4

down the ducal title, his eccentric maternal grandfather had given Cressmouth a reason to thrive.

From Benjamin, he had only taken things away.

It was past time to take his birthright back. He was here for his mother's locket. The one meant for him. The one bearing a miniature family portrait inside, painted mere weeks after Benjamin was born.

It was the only portrait he shared with his mother. She had died shortly after his birth. That had been Benjamin's first Christmastide. That time of the year had not improved since.

After all these years, it finally seemed possible to retrieve the stolen necklace. Benjamin had begged for its safe return a thousand times. But his grandfather was as immovable as his castle.

The old man always said he'd give the golden locket back to Benjamin over his dead body, and the blackguard clearly meant it. He was dead now. Time for the heirloom to come home.

Benjamin shook off the ghost of his grandfather's memory as he alighted outside the castle's doors. A stream of dapper footmen flowed out to greet him.

Murmurs immediately erupted from a growing crowd of onlookers.

"Why, it's the Duke of Silkridge!"

"Happy Christmas, Your Grace!"

"It's *January*," Benjamin growled.

He entrusted his carriage and horses to his driver and the footmen, and made his way inside to see if there was room for him in the castle's crumbling interior.

As he crossed the threshold, Benjamin stared about in disbelief.

The interior was the opposite of crumbling. By all appearances, the abandoned medieval castle had been restored to its former glory and beyond.

In the reception hall, crackling fires roared behind their grates, their orange light dancing over a spotless lake of white marble.

Strips of bright blue carpet guided visitors from the door to any number of destinations. An adjoining salon filled with voices and laughter. A great winding stone staircase led from one sprawling floor to the next.

At a large buffet, footmen cheerfully handed out plates of biscuits and generous ladles of steaming mulled wine. The butler pointed him in that direction after accepting his greatcoat and top hat.

Benjamin didn't want warm, sugary biscuits. He wanted a room for the night, he wanted his mother's locket, and he wanted to be gone.

Before he could have any of these things however, he caught sight of golden blond hair and laughing brown eyes. Just like that, his world tilted on its axis.

Noelle was here. *Right* here.

His heart beat uncomfortably fast.

She looked both the same and yet somehow even better than before. Soft curves and gold-rimmed spectacles. Happy and smiling and beautiful. Surrounded by a group of equally cheerful friends.

He'd thought she would be gone. He'd *hoped* she would be gone.

So many years had passed since he'd last seen her. For the longest time, he had expected her to have a Season in the capitol, to take London by storm. Perhaps she had done so, and he had missed it. After all, he spent his days in the House of Lords and his nights in his study.

Perhaps she was now "Lady" or "Mrs." and no longer the Miss Noelle Pratchett he remembered.

He didn't want details, he reminded himself. Learning she'd found someone else would serve no purpose, and discovering she was still unwed would not signify. And yet he couldn't help but gaze at her hungrily as she broke from her friends and made her way to the refreshment table, right in his direction.

The moment she caught sight of him, she pulled up short. All traces of laughter disappeared from her eyes. "Silkridge."

"Miss Pratchett," he replied, bracing himself for the inevitable correction.

It did not come.

"Five years," she said instead.

"You look lovely," he blurted out, and could have kicked himself. She did look lovely. He had not meant to notice, much less give any compliments.

She ignored it. Her lips pursed. "I thought I would never see you again."

"So did I," he admitted. He had missed her so much, those first few months.

After that, he had done his best to push her from his mind. One should not dwell upon things one could not have. Such as a rekindled romance.

Or forgiveness.

She crossed her arms beneath her bosom. "No doubt you're here for the will."

Ten o'clock on the morrow. He wouldn't be a single moment late.

"I shall be gone before you know it," he promised.

"No doubt." Her smile didn't reach her eyes. "You were last time, too."

CHAPTER 2

*H*e was back.

Noelle Pratchett gazed at the imposing, impossibly handsome gentleman before
her in disbelief. For years, she had vowed that if
she ever crossed paths with the Duke of Silkridge
again, he deserved nothing less than the cut direct.

And yet she was rooted in place. Her knees
were locked tight to keep from trembling and her
traitorous eyes could not be distracted from his
form.

Tall, intense, tightly controlled. It wasn't just
that his clothing had been perfectly tailored to his
lean, muscular body. Every thread, every stitch
had been selected with the same care and preci-
sion that ruled the rest of his life.

He was never well-dressed; he was *perfectly*
dressed. Every fold of his cravat, a work of art.
Every crease, starched and crisp. Every hair just
so, with nary a tendril out of place. His jaw,
smooth and clear of stubble.

He wasn't a fashion plate come to life. The

duke was no dandy. Rather, he was the very embodiment of rules and expectations. His hair, the perfect length. His waistcoat, the ideal pattern. His choices in color and style, muted but elegant. Timeless. As if an artist might paint his portrait at any moment.

And this magic, despite having just stepped inside from a long drive on a blustery day. Not even wrinkles would dare to mar the plans of the Duke of Silkridge.

He was not here for her, of course. For a while —a very short while—her naïve heart had once believed such a thing possible.

Back in those days, he was not yet a duke but rather *Benjamin*. Irresistible, despite the same haunted eyes and carefully controlled exterior. If it had not been for that one reckless kiss, she would not have believed passion capable of sneaking past his defenses.

At the time, she had been delighted. It was a fairy story. She, the penniless orphan. He, the handsome prince. What had begun as friendship had turned into so much more. He would not have kissed her otherwise. Surely this meant they had a future.

He had been horrified. They had no future at all. Indeed, the next morning he was in the first coach leaving Cressmouth. That was the last time she saw him.

Until now.

"This is a surprise," came the duke's low, comforting voice. "I didn't expect to see you."

Noelle was not comforted. She was annoyed. She hadn't *wished* to see him.

The time for girlish innocence had long since passed. She had learned her lesson well. If you open your heart, you will be left behind. She would not make such a foolish mistake again.

The duke accepted two mugs of mulled wine from a passing footman and offered one to her.

Noelle had come to the refreshment table in search of biscuits, not wine, but she supposed now was an excellent time to change her mind.

She accepted the warm mug and allowed its fragrant steam to bathe her face. "Is Christmas as you remember it?"

"Cressmouth," he corrected immediately with no attempt to mask a light shudder. "I don't know how anyone could live here."

Her spine straightened. She loved the village. Loved the people, loved the scenery, loved being wanted. That he felt himself above all of that, including her, made her vow to be Christmassier than ever just to vex him.

"I wish it would snow year-round in all of England, not just here," Noelle replied cheerfully. She gestured about the great hall. "Nothing could be merrier than a cold crisp day outside and a crackling fire inside, especially when surrounded by so many friends."

He did not look convinced. "I don't recognize anyone here but you."

Unsurprising. Silkridge hadn't spent any significant amount of time here since he was a child.

During his most recent visit—five years ago—he had spent a fortnight almost exclusively in Noelle's company. At first, they had thought their friendship was deepening. During a long moonlit stroll, they'd discovered the connection between them was so much more. That perfect, magical night had culminated with their mouths meeting in a kiss. Of course, he would remember such a moment.

It was unforgettable.

"I suppose this party is in Grandfather's honor?" Silkridge gestured at the long buffet piled with refreshments.

"Not at all," she said, infusing her voice with even higher spirits than normal. "You're looking at the spirit of Christmas. The castle offers libations to weary travelers year-round."

He stared at her. "Biscuits are not the spirit of Christmas."

"How would you know, when you don't have any?" she asked.

His blue eyes narrowed. "Biscuits or Christmas spirit?"

"You appear to be sadly in want of both." She took a sip of the spiced wine. Its warmth was just what she needed. It tasted like home. "The castle's kitchen boasts the finest cooks in the region. These biscuits have no equal, and the rest of the meals are every bit as sumptuous. You will not easily find more accommodating footmen or a more thoughtful and efficient maid staff. *This* is the spirit of Christmas."

His skepticism was obvious. "Cressmouth barely holds a thousand souls. Where would

Grandfather even find such a quantity to employ?"

"You said it yourself. Right here in the village. Most of us worked either for your grandfather or for the castle in some capacity."

He looked at her sharply. "You *work*?"

Noelle raised her cup to her mouth. She had not meant to give him any personal details about herself at all.

Especially not information that highlighted the unbridgeable distance between them. To those of his class, "work" was a filthy word fit only for commoners. But here in Cressmouth, work was something everyone did together, making each day even better than the last.

"Noelle," came a breathless voice from just behind her. "Have you seen the duke?"

Silkridge stiffened in affront, no doubt because he was standing within arm's reach of both Noelle and the speaker.

"Not you," she murmured under her breath, then turned to her bosom friend Virginia. "Have you checked the amphitheater? They are setting up for *The Winter's Tale*, and you know how he loves those props."

"You are brilliant," Virginia gushed. "Of course that is where he must be."

She dashed off before Noelle could introduce her to Silkridge. Not that Noelle had any particular wish to ingratiate the duke with her friends. Besides, he would be gone on the morrow. He wasn't here to make friends.

Nonetheless, she performed the niceties.

"That was Miss Virginia Underwood. It is a wonder robins and song thrushes don't follow her about, singing on her shoulders. She is one of the kindest and sweetest people in all of Christmas."

He frowned. "She mentioned a duke?"

"You are not the only one," Noelle said. Her attention was caught by another familiar face.

"Noelle, you've outdone yourself." Angelica Parker lifted a china tea plate towering with biscuits. "I could subsist on the cinnamon ones for the rest of my life."

Silkridge choked in disbelief. "Noelle Pratchett is the castle cook?"

Angelica laughed. "Even better. She is the grand architect that made these biscuits possible. Without her, one might as well be greeted with gruel."

"Grand architect?" The duke blinked in confusion. "What is that supposed to mean?"

But Angelica was already gone, and Noelle didn't feel like explaining. The less he knew about her life, the better. The lives of her friends were a much safer topic.

"Miss Parker has the steadiest hand and keenest eye in all of Christmas. I once saw her create an intricate, jewel-encrusted tiara fit for royalty. You should see it."

He lifted his brows. "I find that jewel-encrusted tiaras tend to unseat one's top hat."

No. She would not find him amusing. That path only led to heartbreak.

"There you are," came another familiar voice.

This one belonged to Olive Harper. "Azureford won't stop pestering me about my stallions."

"Azureford the *duke*?" Silkridge said in obvious befuddlement. "The Duke of Azureford?"

"I told you," Noelle reminded him. "You're not the only duke in Christmas."

She turned to her friend. "You need an auction, of course. Don't allow him to be the only bidder."

Olive pulled a face. "I haven't time to plan an auction. The stable roof needs to be patched and one of my broodmares is looking breach—"

"I'll organize it," Noelle said immediately. "You look after your horses and I will look after the auction."

"Noelle, would you? I shall owe you any favor you wish." Olive squeezed her hand and then dashed toward the door.

A frown marred Silkridge's ducal brow. Either Christmas familial informality or talk of a breach broodmare had met with his disapproval.

He cocked an eyebrow in Noelle's direction. "Do you allow everyone to address you by your Christian name?"

"Not everyone," she said sweetly. "You may call me Miss Pratchett."

A muscle worked in his temple.

"That was a dear friend of mine," she continued as if his question had never been spoken. "Miss Harper has a quick mind, an enormous heart, and one of the most sought-after stud farms in all of England. She is a fascinating woman and a wonderful person."

Silkridge seemed amused by this explanation.

"You make it sound like everyone in Cressmouth is a fine soul and perfect neighbor."

"Possibly because everyone in Cressmouth *is* a fine soul and perfect neighbor," Noelle agreed. She arched her eyebrows right back at him. "That is, almost everyone."

She knew she was being prickly. But sometimes the only way to protect oneself was to keep a safe distance from those who could inflict hurt.

Unfortunately, she was no longer certain such a distance existed between her and Silkridge. His presence on the same mountaintop was more than enough to send her heart racing.

"Will you be attending the reading of Grandfather's last will and testament?" he inquired.

"Most of the village will be attending," she said noncommittally. "Your grandfather meant everything to Christmas."

"He's gone." The duke's expression shuttered. "You can stop calling it 'Christmas.'"

"Mr. Marlowe was the village's savior, not its dictator," she snapped. "He didn't just rename us. He gave us Christmas every day."

Noelle could swear the duke muttered *humbug* under his breath.

"Then I suppose I will see you tomorrow?" he asked aloud.

Not if she could help it seemed a churlish reply.

"I expect the castle to be packed with people," she said instead. "There will be refreshments after, of course."

He shook his head. "Not for me. By then I'll be on my way back to London."

Of course he would. Their hours were already numbered.

Her lips tightened. She should not even be speaking to him. Having him at arm's reach, knowing his presence was only temporary, dredged up all the old feelings, the hackles, the shields. This was not a reunion. It was a brief, chance encounter between former acquaintances who had once shared an equally brief kiss.

If he would not stay for her before, the promise of a refreshment table clearly would not be enough to tempt him.

She doubted anything could.

"Enjoy being home," she said. "Christmas hasn't been the same without you."

It had been better. Safer.

She straightened her spine. From now until his departure, she would endeavor to avoid him completely. Seeing him ripped open a scar she had believed long healed.

"Cressmouth is not home," the duke growled. "And don't call it—"

"Happy Christmas!" she chirped as sunnily as possible, then turned her back and walked away with her head held high.

CHAPTER 3

*T*he warm fire crackling in the hearth of Noelle's bedchamber kept the chill of winter safely on the other side of her frosted window panes.

But not even a merry fire could keep her constant thoughts of Silkridge at bay.

Until he had stepped foot inside the castle last night, Noelle had been perfectly content. Not one arrogant London gentlemen in her life appeared to be the ideal number. The sooner he was gone, the better.

This morning, she dressed with extra care. Not because she had any wish to cast a favorable impression upon Silkridge, but because she wished to achieve the opposite effect. They were not compatible in any way. She couldn't trace her parentage back one generation, let alone ten. He believed her a country bumpkin living in some forgotten village? She would prove she didn't need him or pretentious London finery to be happy.

She left her gowns and her riding habits and

her dashing walking dresses in the back of her armoire and cloaked herself in an old day dress four years out of fashion. The last time he had been here, she had worn all her best garments. They had gone riding, taken long walks... she had even hoped for a dance at the upcoming assembly.

It hadn't come. He had left. She wanted no reminders of the foolish girl she had once been.

She adjusted her dowdy gown before the looking-glass. Her neighbors would not judge her for it. Cressmouth's villagers cared more about a person's interior than her exterior.

Noelle's shoulders curved. When it came to her, it was quite possible Silkridge wouldn't notice either aspect. She had spent more time trying *not* to appear as though she'd been obsessing about him, than he had thought of her in five long years.

Disgusted with herself for allowing his presence to affect her thoughts and actions even for a moment, she spun away from her looking-glass and crossed her bedchamber toward the corridor.

She paused with her fingers above the handle. The duke's guest chamber might be near hers. He could be right outside in the corridor.

The topmost floor on the north wing of the castle was reserved for the family. Noelle had earned such a prestigious spot in exchange for her work in the counting house. Silkridge was guaranteed a place due to being born in the right lineage.

If he was standing on the other side of the door, she might be forced to continue on in his company. After all, they were heading to the same place.

Well, wasn't that what her costume was for? She was nothing like his London ladies and had no wish to be. So much the better if he found her forgettable. She was doing her damnedest to scrape him from her mind as well. No—she was succeeding. Beginning here and now.

The only gentlemen who interested her were locals who loved Cressmouth just as much as she did. The Duke of Silkridge simply did not signify.

She wrenched open the door and strode out into the hall.

The only movement was far ahead where a familiar face in a pale indigo gown headed toward the marble stair.

Noelle hurried to catch up.

"Good morning," she said with genuine warmth as she reached Virginia's side. "Did you find your duke?"

"Indeed I did, the incorrigible scamp," Virginia replied with a smile. "Do you ever wish you had been born a bird so that you could soar over Cressmouth and gaze down upon its beauty from high above the rooftops?"

"I must confess the idea had not occurred to me." Noelle fell into step beside her dear friend. Virginia often spoke as if she were in the midst of a half-remembered dream. She was as likely to look for answers in the palm of one's hands than in the pages of a book.

"Can you believe he's gone?" Virginia asked.

Noelle shook her head. Mr. Marlowe had been the heart and soul of Cressmouth. "The village won't be the same without our leader."

Virginia's voice grew distant. "We are all leaders. Each sparrow takes its turn against the winds in order to guide and protect the others."

That... was an extremely Virginia thing to say. Her frequent aphorisms were one of the many reasons Mr. Marlowe had employed her as his personal advisor. Virginia's methods might be odd, but she was indisputably clever.

Noelle plucked a black cat hair from her friends puffed sleeve. "Did you see the *other* duke?"

Virginia's quick eyes locked on hers. "Your duke?"

"Not my duke," Noelle said quickly. "He belongs to London."

"He belongs to England, and England is part of us all," Virginia amended, her tone pensive.

Usually, Virginia's unusual perspective brought nothing but good cheer. Today, however, her words made Noelle's heart hurt. She was uncertain what was more upsetting, the idea that Silkridge still belonged to her a little, or that he belonged to everyone else just as much.

"Do you know where they put him?" she asked quietly. "Is he here in this wing?"

Virginia shook her head. "He was placed on the wrong floor. The maid who prepared a guest chamber for him did not realize he already had a dedicated room somewhere on this wing."

The last door on the left, to be precise.

Noelle wished she did not remember how she had thrown herself into his path time and time again all those years ago. Her cheeks heated in mortification. She would never again allow herself to behave so rashly.

"Was he upset?" she asked.

"Is a badger upset when it rains?" Virginia answered, trailing her fingers lightly on the balustrade as they descended the stairs.

Noelle blinked. "I have no idea."

"Neither do I," Virginia mused. "I should pay more attention."

"Watch your step," Noelle cautioned her. "Pay attention to the stairs."

"It doesn't matter if the maid's mistake upset Silkridge," Virginia decided.

That was an unusual sentiment. Noelle raised her brows. "Because he turned his back on the village and never returned?"

"Because it's already morning, and too late to undo. We may be deeply embarrassed for the castle staff to have treated Mr. Marlowe's grandson like an ordinary guest, but he will be gone in a few hours and no doubt has already put the incident out of his mind."

The only thing Noelle was deeply embarrassed about was the probability that Virginia was right.

Silkridge had put Noelle and the entire village out of his mind easily enough once before. It would take him no time at all to do so again. Her stomach twisted. She tried to shake off her disillusionment.

There was no reason for her heart to feel clutched in ice at the idea of being forgotten again within the week. She knew his inevitable dismissal was coming. That was why she needed to avoid him at all costs. It would not feel as though he were abandoning her a second time if she was the one who kept him at bay.

He wanted to be gone. She wanted him gone. For once, they were in agreement.

"Silkridge looked quite dashing yesterday," Virginia said. "Didn't you think he cut a fine figure?"

"I didn't notice," Noelle said quickly. She could recall every stitch, every smirk, every dismissive comment about Christmas from memory. And she had done so all night long.

"It was the top hat," Virginia decided. "The way it was so perfect, sooty black with a dusting of ice crystals upon the rim, set at just the right rakish angle. Or perhaps it was his cravat. Have you ever seen a knot so intricate? Both elements drew the eye to his face, which I must say is no hardship to gaze upon. Eyes as blue as a great crown crane, cheekbones as—"

"Enough!" Noelle blurted. "I saw him. Fancy ascot. Attractive birdlike eyes. Please don't keep describing him to me."

Virginia narrowed her eyes in consideration. "The two of you would make a striking pair, don't you think?"

"We wouldn't even make it through an afternoon," Noelle said flatly. "He is the last man I'd choose. When I marry, it will be someone who respects me, my village, and everything I love."

"Interesting," Virginia said as if Noelle had helped her to solve a great mystery.

"Interesting that I want a husband who loves and respects me?" she asked dryly.

Virginia's brows arched. "Interesting that when I mention Silkridge, your first thought is marriage."

"He is the embodiment of everything I do not want," Noelle enunciated firmly.

She was in no danger of falling in love with him. Silkridge had not only left her, he had abandoned his own grandfather. That behavior spoke volumes. Noelle rather hoped the duke had been written out of the will completely.

"He hates Christmas," she said. "He's impossible."

"Does he hate *Christmas* or Cressmouth?" Virginia asked.

"Same thing," Noelle answered.

Rejecting Christmas meant rejecting Cressmouth. Rejecting Noelle. She was as much a part of this village and everything it stood for as the mountain breeze that blew through it.

Virginia lifted a shoulder. "Perhaps he has changed."

"He has not," Noelle said. Last night had proven as much. His position on Cressmouth had been clear. "Nor has he given any sign of wishing to bend on the matter."

"Sometimes rigid is good." Virginia's lips curved wickedly.

Noelle slanted her a warning look. "Do not even suggest—"

Virginia blinked innocently. "That nature always finds a way? The woodpecker relies on a beak as hard as stone in order to seek sustenance. Dukes are not so different."

Whatever Virginia meant, Noelle disagreed. Silkridge wasn't seeking anything here, sustenance or otherwise. That was the problem.

She pushed him out of her mind as they reached the bottom of the stair. A queue had formed downstairs in the main corridor. They were early. The doors had not yet been opened to allow in those called for the reading of the will.

"Miss Pratchett and Miss Underwood!" A portly gentleman with white hair and an omnipresent worsted cap atop his head enveloped them in a jovial embrace.

Fred Fawkes was Noelle's mentor, or at least he had been before age had begun to affect his memory and his hearing. Now he went nowhere without a trusty ear trumpet clutched in one hand.

"Good to see you, Mr. Fawkes," she shouted into the ear trumpet. "You are looking handsome as ever today."

She was never sure if he completely understood the things she shouted into his ear, but she did her best to include him all the same. He had been Mr. Marlowe's clerk for decades. One could be forgiven for thinking Mr. Fawkes as responsible for turning Cressmouth into Christmas as his old master had been.

Noelle did her best to be just as indispensable. Mr. Marlowe was gone, and Mr. Fawkes was no longer a clerk, which meant Noelle was now the lynchpin of the counting house.

Or at least, she had been until now. She did not think Mr. Marlowe's will and testament would strip her from her post, but she could not be certain whether the will had been revised recently enough to include her.

The doors opened, and the queue streamed from the corridor into a large chamber with hundreds of chairs.

"Now, Miss Pratchett." Mr. Fawkes pinched her cheek. "I must ask you to mind the counting house for me while I attend the reading of Marlowe's will."

"I have been attending to the counting house since you retired four years ago," she reminded him as gently as one could whilst screaming into an ear trumpet. "All of Cressmouth is under the castle roof attending the same reading."

Mr. Fawkes looked startled. "Is that so? When do the proceedings start?"

Noelle hooked her arm through his and led him into the crowded chamber. "At this very moment."

CHAPTER 4

*W*hen Benjamin arrived downstairs
for the reading of the will, he was
already in a restless mood.

It had begun last night when he was shown to a
recently renovated bedchamber in an unfamiliar
part of the castle. Though the room and its fire
were welcoming, he could not help but feel a
stranger in a place where he had spent a good part
of his childhood.

The feeling had not abated. He had tossed and
turned, torn between his anger toward his grandfather and the wholly unacceptable rush of
longing he felt every time he thought of Noelle.
Cressmouth was torture.

He was glad this particular trial was almost
over. Scant moments remained. Sit through a
short reading, collect the locket, be on his way.

At least, that was what he had expected prior to
finding himself in an enormous chamber stuffed
with countless spectators. Despite what appeared
to be the presence of hundreds of chairs, that op-

portunity had vanished long before Benjamin had entered the room. He was forced to stand with his back against the wainscoting like a wallflower at her first dance.

"Why is the solicitor primping on a dais in a ballroom as if this were a stage?" he growled to the person next to him.

Belatedly, he recognized the woman as the jeweler who made tiaras fit for royalty, not that there could be much call for extravagance in the middle of nowhere.

Benjamin wished he hadn't recognized her at all. No good could come of making personal connections with the villagers. He would be leaving them behind within the hour.

Leaving Noelle behind was hard enough.

"This village loves the stage," the jeweler replied cryptically.

He snorted. "All the world's a stage, and the inhabitants merely players?"

"Shakespeare." The jeweler inclined her head. "Very nice. Mr. Fawkes would be proud."

Benjamin perked up despite himself. The castle clerk had been dearer to him than his own grandfather.

He scanned the room in vain. "All these people cannot possibly be named in the will."

"We are," the jeweler answered with pride. "Mr. Marlowe would never forget one of his flock."

Benjamin shot her a wry glance. "Because my grandfather was such a good shepherd?"

"Because he loved a menagerie," she corrected

with a grin. "He would have turned this castle into a circus if Mr. Fawkes would have let him."

Benjamin was unsurprised to hear that his eccentric grandfather had not become any less odd with age. Nor was he surprised that this characteristic should be met with an indulgent smile and nostalgic tone of voice. Grandfather had been devoted to Cressmouth, and Cressmouth alone.

He was saved from this line of thought by a glimpse of golden blonde hair. Noelle was here.

Of course she would be. The entire village was here. But they were not the ones who made his heart beat faster and his mind empty of reason.

She looked just as beautiful in the morning sun as she had by candlelight the evening before. Even more beautiful, if such a thing were possible. He should look away. And he would, any moment now.

He loved the way she wrinkled her nose any time her gold-rimmed spectacles started to slide. He loved the way she laughed, the way her whole face lit up, the way joy seemed to emanate from her entire body. Not that he could see much of it. She was surrounded by friends and well-wishers.

Benjamin was a moth drawn to her flame, but this community was her butterflies. Colorful and energetic where he was distant and staid. Cressmouth was where and how she thrived. Noelle did not need him disrupting her happy life.

He wished he had not run into her. It would have been easier for them both if he had glimpsed her from afar and slipped away with her none the wiser. Now that he had seen her, had spoken to her, he should let that be enough.

But his feet were moving in her direction as though logic held no sway.

Imbecile. He wasn't edging sideways through a packed crowd just to be closer to a woman who distrusted him, he told himself. He had simply noticed that Noelle stood directly beside Mr. Fawkes, who Benjamin was thrilled to see still grumpy and kicking.

When he got within shouting distance, Mr. Fawkes and another older gentleman were too engrossed in a lively conversation about the causes and treatments of gout to notice Benjamin's arrival.

Noelle, however, noticed right away.

He could tell by the way her stance stiffened.

"Can the Duke of Silkridge be heading straight for Miss Pratchett?" came a loud whisper.

"Fret not," Noelle assured her friend. "My gaze cannot be turned by London gentlemen."

But her eyes had not left Benjamin.

"What's so wonderful about Cressmouth lads?" he asked as he reached her side.

She narrowed her eyes as if mentally preparing for battle. "They can be counted upon to be here every day, not to give a girl bad dreams at night."

"You dreamt about me," he said with pleasure. At least he was not alone.

"*Bad* dreams," she reminded him. "Ghastly."

His smile faded. He deserved that. She knew as well as he did that if he could be trusted to do one thing, anything, that thing would be to leave.

At least there was honesty between them.

He wished there were also about a hundred fewer spectators. He wished a lot of things.

But he was a man of reason and practicality, not poetry and love. Benjamin's priorities had been predetermined. A duke served his country, not himself. Noelle was not part of the equation. He absolutely shouldn't be fascinated by the wrinkle of her nose or the way her lips pursed to one side when she was thinking.

If the two of them were too different before, the chasm was now impossible. She *was* Cressmouth. She was not for him at all.

He forced himself to tear his gaze from Noelle and concentrate instead on Grandfather's clerk, Mr. Fawkes. Mr. Fawkes still wore that oversized worsted cap, every bit as white and fuzzy as the shock of hair it attempted to corral beneath.

His beard was longer than Benjamin recalled, his cheeks ruddier, his eyes just as sparkly. Seeing him was as if no time had passed at all.

Mr. Fawkes caught a glimpse of Benjamin and broke off the discussion of gout at once.

Benjamin grinned despite himself. It was good to see the old man. "Mr. Fawkes! You haven't aged a day."

"Who's this lad?" Mr. Fawkes demanded to Noelle. "He looks familiar."

Benjamin froze in shock and hurt. Perhaps the years hadn't been so kind after all.

"The Duke of Silkridge," Noelle replied loudly.

Mr. Fawkes furrowed his brow. "Scrooge, you say?"

Benjamin gaped at him. "What the devil is a 'scrooge?'"

"*Silkridge*," she shouted into his ear. "Where's your ear trumpet?"

"You must be mistaken." Mr. Fawkes lifted an ivory-and-silver horn to the side of his head. "The Duke of Silkridge passed away years ago."

"His son," Noelle said into the ear trumpet. "Benjamin. The heir."

Mr. Fawkes's face lit up. "Oh, of course. Why didn't you say?"

Noelle gave a quick curtsey in apology.

Benjamin stepped forward, relieved to have been recognized at last.

"I—" he began.

But Mr. Fawkes did not hear him.

"Suppose you are wanting to know what could bring down an crotchety buzzard like your grandfather," Mr. Fawkes said with a hacking laugh.

Benjamin had no wish for a detailed accounting. "I—"

"Quincy," Mr. Fawkes continued unabated. "Spent weeks with poultices wrapped about his head. Looked like an Egyptian mummy, he did. Except for the size of his neck and chin and tongue. Swelled right up after that abscess on his gum. I'm thinking of having every one of my teeth pulled to be safe."

"Have you enough to bother?" cackled the gentleman who had been debating gout remedies moments earlier.

"Good point," Mr. Fawkes said, slapping his knee. He turned back to Benjamin. "A man must do *something* to prepare for his eventuality, wouldn't you say?"

Benjamin swallowed. "I…"

"This lad takes more precautions than most," Mr. Fawkes boomed to his companion. "Can't blame him. His sire also died during Christmastide. He suffered the ague. Virulent strain even quinine couldn't cure."

This time, Benjamin didn't try to speak. He couldn't. The breath had been robbed from his lungs at the reminder of his loss.

All Christmastide had ever done was steal family members from him. Father's loss had nearly broken him. Becoming duke was easy. Duke was merely a job, a task to perform. But Benjamin had not been ready to lose another parent.

Mr. Fawkes's companion lifted a quizzing glass and squinted at Benjamin. "Didn't the old duke have black hair?"

"That he did," Mr. Fawkes agreed. "My lad here takes after his mother in that regard."

Each word sliced open old wounds.

Everyone Grandfather's age remembered Benjamin's mother. They could tell at a glance which parts of him reminded them of her.

He could not. His grandfather had absconded with the only heirloom he had ever cared about. The one with the portrait of Benjamin's mother inside.

Mr. Fawkes used his ear trumpet to gesture toward Benjamin. "My lad here is the last of his line on his mother's side."

That was why he needed the locket. He tried not

to clench his fists at the unwelcome reminder. This quest wasn't just a matter of retrieving something that was lost, but a chance to get his family back. If only as painted miniatures hanging about his neck.

He tried to swallow, but his throat was too tight. How he had hated being estranged from his grandfather. He missed having a family. Would have visited as often as he could if it were possible to be cordial.

It had not been possible. Benjamin's birth had caused his mother's death, and Grandfather had never forgiven him for the loss. He had turned all his love to Cressmouth instead. For Benjamin, there had only been coldness.

Grandfather had once snarled that he would rather have lost his grandchild than his daughter. What use was a baby? She could always have another. Or at least, she might have, had she recovered from Benjamin's difficult birth.

After realizing the depth of his grandfather's hatred, Benjamin had taken his words to heart. He would be as useful as ten dukes. He would make the House of Lords his family, his home, his reason for being. He would not limit his responsibilities to one small village but rather the whole of England. Perhaps in doing so, Benjamin could make his mother's sacrifice worth it.

"Well," Mr. Fawkes's gouty companion said with a smile. "At least Your Grace is still kicking. That makes it a happy Christmas, I say."

"There's nothing happy about Christmas," Benjamin said flatly.

He hadn't expected Mr. Fawkes to overhear him, but the man's eyes had been following Benjamin's lips close. "Now, lad, it isn't all bad. What about the title? You inherited a dukedom."

"And lost my family," Benjamin pointed out. It would be better *not* to love than to have someone unexpectedly ripped from one's life.

"True." Mr. Fawkes leaned forward to pat Benjamin on the forearm in sympathy.

Before Benjamin could answer, the growing crowd of onlookers could not hold their tongues any longer. They interrupted Mr. Fawkes like a basket of kittens, tumbling over each other to present themselves to Benjamin. Before he could object, he was swept away from Noelle and into their midst.

"Your grandfather was the loveliest man I ever met," said a stout woman in a flour-dusted apron. "Christmas wouldn't exist without him."

"Cressmouth," Benjamin corrected firmly. "Let us not overstate the matter."

"He gave me a post when others would not," said a young girl with a scarred face.

"That's because they're foolish where you're from," said the woman in the apron. "Mr. Marlowe wasn't foolish."

"Not one bit," agreed a gentleman leaning on a cane. "Why, without him there wouldn't be an annual biscuit festival."

"Annual biscuit festival," Benjamin echoed, deadpan. "He *did* invent Christmas."

"What was it like?" asked a stableboy breathlessly. "To have a grandfather as wonderful as Mr. Marlowe?"

"What do you suppose it was like?" A man with dirt-stained fingers cuffed the lad on the back of the head. "A miracle, no doubt."

"A marvelous influence, I reckon," a different woman piped in. "His Grace is known as the most powerful lord in parliament. When the crown needs something done, they put the Duke of Silkridge in charge. Who does that sound like, if not our Mr. Marlowe?"

Benjamin ground his teeth. It did not sound like his grandfather at all.

It sounded like a duke who gave up sleep, gave up hobbies, gave up every spare moment he ever had for the betterment of his country. It sounded like skipped meals and ink-stained fingers. It sounded like audiences before the Regent and im-passioned speeches to the House of Lords. It sounded like someone who didn't have time for playing at Christmas because he was too busy doing his part to keep England safe and secure for the people in this room and every other corner of the country.

Grandfather hadn't been there for any of it.

"Why is Mr. Marlowe's grandson on his feet?" someone yelled.

"A chair, if you please!" someone else called out. "Mr. Marlowe's grandson needs a seat!"

Benjamin could not believe the reasoning. Here in Cressmouth, he was famous not for being a duke, but for being related to his irascible grandfather.

A young lady popped up from her chair. "You can have mine."

"I'll stand," he bit out. "I will not steal a lady's seat."

"I knew you wouldn't," she said with a self-satisfied smile. "When it is his turn to do so, the sparrow always leads into the wind."

Benjamin stared at her more closely. "Weren't you the young lady hunting for a duke?"

She nodded. "I found him prancing between the verdant tree and fake bear, as a duke is wont to do."

He blinked. "I vow that I have never in my life—"

"You are not the only duke in Christmas," she said vaguely.

"So I've gathered." He couldn't be gone quickly enough. "I suppose there are two of us, then? Perhaps three?"

"There are twelve dukes in Christmas." She cast a proud glance toward her neighbor as if to verify such an absurd claim.

"Twelve dukes of Christmas?" he repeated in disbelief.

Bloody hell, she had actually gotten him to say Christmas instead of Cressmouth.

"It's too bad Tiny Tim isn't a duke," murmured her neighbor. "Then we could have thirteen."

"You're absolutely right," said another. "I suppose we have Mr. Marlowe to blame for that."

It was all Benjamin could do to keep his head from exploding. He was not going to ask who Tiny Tim was, and he definitely wasn't going to ask what on earth his maternal grandfather had to do with anyone becoming a duke. Benjamin's title had been the last gift from his father. Grandfather had given him nothing but heartache.

A gong sounded on the side of the dais and then the solicitor took center stage.

"Shh!" Several ladies shushed the crowd. "The reading is about to start."

Thank God. Benjamin forced his tense shoulders to relax. In a matter of hours, his carriage would be leaving Cressmouth and he could return to real life.

"We are gathered here today," the solicitor began, "for a reading of the last will and testament of our beloved Mr. Jacob Marlowe, who rescued our failing village and established Christmas in its place. Would anyone like to begin with a few words?"

No. No words. Benjamin tried not to groan audibly. There were a few hundred people stuffed into this ballroom. If everyone said a "few" words, the reading wouldn't be over until nightfall.

Yet he had no choice but to stand there and listen.

To his surprise, the heartfelt speeches indicated that the village did not revere his grandfather as an exemplar of excellence. They simply revered him, oddities and all.

Apparently, in addition to the absurd idea of establishing a village dedicated to celebrating Christmastide year-round, Grandfather had had thousands of other eccentric notions. Plans that the villagers had found creative ways to indefinitely postpone.

Preparing a place from which to launch a hot air balloon for when dirigibles became *de rigueur*.

Requiring the kitchen to dye all food the colors of the flag to show support of Britain's efforts against Napoleon.

Installing water tunnels to turn the castle into a circus, complete with tightrope walkers above a pit of crocodiles.

Good lord. Turning Cressmouth into Christmas was perhaps the sanest of all his grandfather's mad schemes.

"Was he in his right mind?" Benjamin asked the older woman to his left in wonder.

"He was a jolly, mischievous fool," she replied with damp eyes. "I shouldn't be surprised if his will is full of more of the same."

A mischievous fool. Iron encased Benjamin's heart. If he had been summoned all the way to the northernmost peak of England a few days before Parliament was set to start anew, only because his grandfather found it *amusing* to manipulate emotions even after his death—

"And now for the reading of the will," announced the solicitor.

Benjamin listened in growing trepidation as it seemed like every person in the room was named before him. His stomach tightened. If he had come all this way, only to learn that his grandfather had buried himself with the locket as a final insult—

"—and to my grandson, Benjamin Ward, Duke of Silkridge, Earl of…"

Benjamin's head snapped up.

The solicitor cleared his throat. "'Be changed or be cursed. This is your last chance.'"

"Oh, for the love of…" Benjamin ground his teeth.

Of course, Grandfather would choose melodrama in favor of plain English. Mischievous fool indeed.

It was all he could do not to yell, *skip to the part where my mother's heirloom returns to me.*

The villagers wouldn't understand. He doubted they knew the locket existed or would care even if they did. It was of value to no living person besides Benjamin, who was tired of waiting. He had suffered more than enough Christmas *and* Cressmouth for the rest of his life. As soon as the locket was in his hand, he would leave this place and never look back.

The solicitor continued, "'You must complete the renovations on my unfinished aviary.'"

"Complete the what on his what?" Benjamin spluttered in disbelief. "He isn't granting me a bequest. He's asking for a favor. Is that even legal?"

He should not have expected better, and yet he was still bitterly disappointed.

"'—I do not grant Silkridge the privilege of populating the aviary with an appropriate collection of birds—'"

"Thank God," Benjamin muttered.

"'—but in order for restorations to be considered complete, Silkridge must open a ceremonial bottle of champagne upon its threshold before witnesses—'"

"'*Sabrage?*' I'm to slice the bottle open with a saber, just as Napoleon does when conquering new territories?" Benjamin gaped through the crowd at the solicitor in disbelief. "Shall I design a colonial flag for the aviary as well? What kind of daft restorations are these?"

"—and stock the interior with its first symbolic bird, which must be a—"

"Dodo?" Benjamin guessed. "Raptor? African swallow?"

"—partridge."

Benjamin blinked. He was to break a bottle of wine upon the helm of a landlocked aviary in order to present all and sundry with their first ceremonial… partridge? His teeth clenched.

Of course he was.

"The aviary must open within a month of this reading," the solicitor concluded. "Silkridge must remain on premises until that date, or else forfeit forever the gold locket currently held in trust."

"Are you *bamming* me?" Benjamin's blood heated. "I don't have a month before the new session of Parliament. I have less than a fortnight."

The elderly woman patted his arm. "Where there is a will, there's a way."

"That is *not* what that phrase means," he muttered. Where Grandfather was concerned, there was rarely a way.

Muscles tight with anger, Benjamin made his way toward the dais. Grandfather had betrayed him not once but twice, by withholding the locket from its rightful owner first in life and now also in death.

He had obviously taken pleasure in crafting his ridiculous challenge. Benjamin clenched his fists. He hated that his grandfather was making him dance to strings for something that should already be his.

A grandfather was meant to love his grandchild. Not taunt him with the memory of his dead mother.

"Where is it?" he demanded as he stalked to the dais.

The solicitor lowered the papers. "Where is what?"

"The locket," Benjamin growled. "Before I lift a finger, I must verify it still exists and that my grandfather isn't toying with me."

"Mr. Marlowe would never toy with his grandson," chided a kindly voice behind him.

If only that were true.

CHAPTER 5

*A*fter stalking out of the reading of the will, Benjamin did not stay to share refreshments with the rest of the villagers. His appetite had been spoiled, and he certainly didn't feel like sharing stories about his grandfather.

Nor could he return to his cold, impersonal chamber. There was nothing intrinsically wrong with the guest quarters. They had clearly been recently renovated and were spotlessly clean. But a bedchamber was all it was.

If he was going to be trapped here for the next few days, he was going to need an office... Or at the very least, a writing desk and stationery. He must send word to London that he had suffered a brief delay but would still arrive well before Parliament opened to continue policy discussions with his committees.

And then he would do whatever it took to make the aviary halfway presentable and shove a partridge inside so that he could retrieve the locket and be on his way. By tomorrow, if possible.

It all depended on the current state of the aviary's reconstruction.

He caught sight of the lead housekeeper. Perfect. No one would know the castle better.

"May I be of service, Your Grace?" she asked.

"I hope so." He tried his best to mask his impatience with his grandfather's machinations. "Is there an empty study I could use or a desk I might borrow?"

"The counting house," she replied without hesitation. "It was your grandfather's primary study. I am confident you will find all you need there."

Of course. Mr. Fawkes had clerked in the counting house since before Benjamin was born. After seeing the state of his health yesterday, Benjamin had assumed Mr. Fawkes had retired at the same time as Grandfather.

No matter. Even if the room had been untouched for some time, the housekeeper was right. It should contain everything Benjamin might need. At least for such a brief stay.

The counting house might be a small chamber atop the south tower, but in some ways, it was the heart of the castle. That was where all the accounting practices took place. The resident clerks ensured every detail was carefully logged in meticulous journals of accounts. Mr. Fawkes and his books boasted an encyclopedic knowledge of every transaction the castle had ever incurred. The room would be empty, but still be well-stocked with supplies.

Benjamin strode to the south tower and wound his way up to the top of the turret. To his surprise, every wall sconce he passed contained a lit candle.

The pale yellow light did nothing to warm the icy tower. Instead, they cast spidery shadows across the gray stone walls, the dark patterns scurrying and leaping in syncopation with each foot fall on the stairs.

Benjamin had always hated the counting house. Too distant, too dark. Too cold. The claustrophobic stairwell and the cramped little rooms made tales of princesses locked in towers seem more like a Gothic mystery than a fairy story. He could not wait to leave it all behind.

When he reached the top, he shoved open the slender oak door.

His pulse skipped. He was not alone. The queen was in the counting house counting out her money.

Or plotting how to rid the castle of an unwanted duke.

Noelle glanced up from whatever correspondence she'd been writing and froze, plume in hand. "What are *you* doing here?"

"What are *you* doing here?" he countered brilliantly. She had always managed to wipe all intelligent words from his mind.

At first, he did not notice her lack of response because he was too busy drinking in every aspect of her person.

The gold-rimmed spectacles were perched on the tip of her pert nose. Her coif, a loose twist. Half a dozen soft tendrils fell against her slender neck or kissed the side of her cheeks. Even scowling at him, she was a vision. His heart thumped.

How he wanted to brush those soft tendrils from her face with the pad of his thumb and lower his mouth to—

"I work here," she said, her voice remarkably even for a woman who likely wished to stab him with the quill in her hand.

He had never apologized for leaving. To do so, he would have to explain emotions he preferred to bury. Like why he could not bear another attachment… and another loss. The fissures she created in the shields around his heart were a liability.

He had not wished to hurt her by leaving. But it had been kinder to leave when all they'd shared was a single kiss. Prolonging the inevitable would have been much crueler. For both of them.

This time, Benjamin would keep his distance.

"If you worked for my grandfather, why are you still here?" He glanced about the otherwise empty room. Being one of Grandfather's secretaries sounded like torture.

"Why wouldn't I be?" She glanced up from her correspondence. "Mr. Marlowe didn't sack me. He died."

"Shouldn't whoever is in charge of the counting house be going through the journals and completing documents?"

He realized his mistake as soon as the words were out of his mouth.

"You work here," he said before she could reply. "You took Mr. Fawkes's place."

"That's right." She bit her lip. "He helped me

during the transition. His mind is sharper than his hearing."

Benjamin nodded. "I don't doubt it."

A new silence fell, different than before. Worse, he realized. Noelle was no longer expecting him to apologize for the past. She assumed he wasn't going to.

He wished he could. That there was anything at all that could excuse his absence. From the first, he had enjoyed her company far more than he should.

By the time he'd learned she was an orphan far below his class, it no longer mattered. They were already inseparable. *Too* inseparable. Their friendship would have challenged Society more than enough. Their single stolen kiss had been so dramatically outside his control that it had sent him reeling. Retreat was the only safe path for them both.

Gingerly, he stepped into the counting house and seated himself behind the great mahogany desk that had once belonged to his grandfather.

The only items in the room were his large desk, her small desk, a bookshelf, and a pitiful fire spitting orange behind the grate. They were alone.

Very, very alone.

He cleared his throat. "Should you summon a maid?"

She raised her brows. "To watch over me sitting in my chair at my desk as I perform the duties of my post, as I've done alone every day for the last four years?"

Fair enough. Yet they could not continue like this.

He tried again. "Should *I* summon a maid?"

"You're not going to kiss me, much less compromise me," she said flatly. "Should you working at your desk whilst I work at mine raise any eyebrows, I preemptively decline any resulting marriage proposal. I would prefer to remain a spinster."

That was clear enough.

Benjamin broke her gaze in order to rummage through drawers and pigeonholes for supplies. He found ink and wax. But peace of mind was nowhere to be found.

Being forced to face the woman he had hurt was hell. Especially because he could not make things better or change the past. He wouldn't if he could. Leaving had been the right choice. And going back in time to erase their stolen kiss... Even he could not bring himself to do that.

Before he dipped his quill in ink, he slid her another glance from the corner of his eye. Something was different. Something important. It wasn't her looks; she would be beautiful no matter what she wore. His gut clenched. It was what was missing.

Her smile.

He had never seen her without it for this long. It was one of the first things that had attracted him to her. One of the many reasons he had not wished to disappoint her with a goodbye. Even this morning, she had been in good humor, laughing with her friends.

Granted, he could not count himself amongst that number, but the chilliness emanating from her corner of the room was even frostier than the weather outside.

"Did something happen?" he asked.

"Something happened," she agreed. "You didn't stay for the remainder of the reading?"

"I couldn't." He would not explain the spiral of anger and frustration his grandfather's final game had caused. Even now, he could not be certain that dancing to the old man's tune would result in anything at all. Yet he had to try. "What other tricks did Grandfather leave behind?"

Her expression was grim. "His will instructed me to remain as clerk and personal advisor to you during the reconstruction of the aviary."

"You're my personal advisor," he repeated. What the devil was Grandfather about this time?

She appeared as thrilled as Benjamin was about this new development, which was not at all. "Only for a month, until you open the aviary or leave."

"In exchange for what?" he asked suspiciously

"In exchange for nothing." She shrugged. "Those are simply his wishes."

He stared at her. "But you don't have to follow them. Not if there's no bequest hanging in the balance."

"There is a bequest. He has provided me with a generous dowry. It simply is not contingent on any particular constraints. I *choose* to follow his wishes."

Even if it means time spent with you went unspoken.

Benjamin did not ask why her bequest had come freely and his had not. Grandfather was capricious in many ways, but with Benjamin he had always been consistent.

"It won't be a month," he promised her. "My presence is required in the House of Lords within a fortnight. This won't take long. I'll employ as many workers as it takes to complete the aviary as quickly as possible. First I will need to make inquiries into what's been done, what's still needed, and where one might find materials and labor nearby."

She laid the letter she had been writing atop similar such documents, tapped them into a neat rectangle, and extended the stack toward Benjamin.

"What's this?" he asked.

She did not respond.

He reached across the desk to accept the stack. His eyes widened in surprise as he riffled quickly through the pages. "This is a detailed summary of the original plans, all completed construction, all pending restorations, workers' names, directions, and wages... and the location of the outbuilding containing all necessary material."

"Yes." She set down her quill. "Everything you need should be in those documents."

She'd gathered all that information in the space of hours? For him? He gaped at her. "How did you... Why did you..."

"It's not a favor," she reminded him. "I'm your clerk and personal advisor until you open the aviary or leave, whichever comes first."

He managed not to wince at the implied rebuke. "Are you going to be here in the counting house every day?"

She arched a brow. "Performing my assigned duties and respecting a dying man's final wishes?"

"A simple 'yes' would do," he muttered. Of course she would be here.

He was stuck, but so was she. Even if Benjamin managed to find some other study to work in, Noelle would feel honor-bound to present herself each day as his clerk and personal advisor. There was no way out. They would be staring across these desks at each other until further notice.

He flipped through her documentation again, slower this time. It was good work. Clean and comprehensive. She had shaved entire days from the challenge just by offering him such a wealth of information. He slid a sidelong glance her way.

She had not known what might be in the will any more than he or anyone else had, which meant she'd had such numbers at her fingertips all along. She didn't just work here. She appeared to be a phenomenal clerk. No doubt she had made an equally impressive personal advisor to his grandfather.

"Is there anything else I should know about?" he asked.

"I took the liberty of moving your assigned guest quarters to a different bedchamber," she said without looking up from whatever journal she was perusing now.

Given her cool feelings toward him, Benjamin could only assume this meant he had been sent to the mews to sleep with the horses. Whatever surprise she had in store for him, at least it would only be temporary.

He dipped his pen in ink. The wise course of action would be to concentrate on the aviary, not on Noelle.

He dashed off a summons along with an offer of increased wages to each of the names on the list. He would gladly pay double to be done with this farce.

According to Noelle's notes, the aviary required little more than window washers and workers to trim the shrubs. His spirits lightened. The reconstruction would not require a fortnight after all. He could be gone in just a few days.

At the thought, his gaze immediately returned to Noelle. Beautiful brown eyes squinted behind thin spectacles. Plump pink lips pursed to one side as she concentrated on whatever she read. Her slender fingers tucked one of her many errant tendrils behind her ear. His pulse beat faster.

Seeing her before him was like inviting a specter into his heart, whisking him back through time to a different day, a different Christmastide, a different spark in the air.

Five years ago, he'd still believed his grandfather might grow to love him. He would never have dreamed that the old man would steal the locket, much less have to die before returning it to Benjamin.

Back then, his father had still been alive. Benjamin was not yet in the House of Lords, not yet spending every waking moment hunched over a desk or shouting at a podium before his peers.

Back then, Benjamin had been naïve enough to believe he could kiss a pretty girl and maybe it would turn to more. That love was something he could keep.

He had learned differently. Nothing good could stay. The only encounters he was meant to have were with those who wanted little from him except what they could have at that very moment. A favor. A kiss. A moment of his attention. Not a lifetime of it.

The Christmas after he'd left Noelle, Father had died. It was the last Christmas Benjamin had acknowledged. He refused to celebrate it... or even admit it existed.

Until now. Until *here*. Until her.

Everything about Noelle reminded him of Cressmouth. Everything about Cressmouth was designed to remind and evoke Christmas. Every-thing about Christmas reminded him of death and loss.

Everyone he had ever cared about had been taken from him. Since childhood, he had lived in terror of losing someone he loved again, until he realized the simple solution. *Don't love.*

Such an ideology might not bring happiness, but nor did it bring despair. In a world where nothing lasted, it was better not to try, not to be disappointed, not to get hurt. He had left her be-cause he had feared being left.

The wise course of action would be to suffer through the next few days with as much distance between them as possible. No matter how pretty she looked in her gold-rimmed spectacles. The more he spent time with Noelle, the harder it would be to go. No sense playing with fire. He should leave their brief connection in the past where it belonged.

But temptation was so hard to fight. She was right *here*, on the other side of the room. A short distance. An eternity this time. When he left Cressmouth, he would not see her again. This was his last chance to gaze upon her face, to hear her voice. To be this close.

He could not bear the silence. But what did they have to talk about, save the shared pain in their past? It would not do at all. He racked his brain for a new topic. A safer topic.

"Did Tiny Tim receive a bequest in the will?" he asked. He had no idea who Tim was, save that the man was rumored to be in want of a duchy.

Noelle stared at him for a long moment, her face devoid of expression. "No. Tiny Tim already embodies the spirit of Christmas. He wants for nothing."

Benjamin could not imagine what that meant. As much as he wished to avoid any conversation that included Christmas, he was more curious about Tiny Tim than ever. Or perhaps it was Noelle who made him curious. The more time he spent with her, the more intriguing she became.

That way lay danger. He should pay attention to the task at hand, not Cressmouth's inhabitants —and definitely not the woman seated across from him.

No matter how tempting he found her.

He forced himself to concentrate on the aviary. "I don't suppose you have a catalogue of all bird purveyors in the region, as well as literature about the ideal feed and habitat conditions of a captured partridge?"

She glanced up. "I can compile it by tomorrow."

Benjamin blinked in surprise. He had been jesting. Noelle clearly was not. He leaned back in his chair. Grandfather might have appointed her to Benjamin's side, but he had no intention of treating her like an employee.

"No need," he assured her. "Partridges are plentiful and research is unnecessary. It's just a bird."

She lifted her shoulder. "I am a competent clerk. I don't mind dealing with the situation concerning the partridge for you."

"It's not a situation," he said. "I myself am quite competent. If I can help run Parliament, I can acquire a partridge."

"As you wish." Her expression was skeptical at best, but she returned her attention to whatever she had been working on without further commentary.

Benjamin tried not to be offended by her obvious lack of confidence in him. He might be out of place in Cressmouth but he was far from helpless. Such a simple project would be completed in no time. He would check the castle cellar for champagne, and stock the aviary with precisely one bird. Easy enough. He did not need her help.

Yet he could not deny his admiration of her organizational skills. The documentation she had prepared on the local workforce had been incredibly thorough. He had no doubt she would be able to deliver just as exhaustive a report on the care and feeding of partridges, the ideal time and place to purchase fowl, and the best ways of encouraging nesting upon arrival. Whatever she thought of him, he did not wish for her to believe a duke might require such molly-coddling. In fact, this was a wonderful opportunity to prove himself.

Due to his estranged relationship with his grandfather, Benjamin had correctly assumed he would neither inherit the castle nor its coin.

Given his grandfather's eccentricities, perhaps Benjamin should not have been surprised to discover the old man had left the castle in trust for the use of the entire village. It belonged to everyone and no one at once; the beating heart of a vibrant community.

Such a philanthropic plan might sound neat and tidy to someone who had never actually had to *manage* a population of any size. Benjamin, however, had spent years dealing with budgets and physical systems and dissenting opinions. Nothing was easy.

No doubt, Grandfather had believed his mad decision to donate the castle to an entire village no more capricious than his decision to squander the Marlowe fortune on the creation of a Christmas village in the first place.

Although Benjamin was unaffected personally by such whimsy—his title and wealth came from his father's side of the family—he could not walk away without assuring himself that Cressmouth wouldn't flounder before the solicitor could make sense of the accounts.

Benjamin let out a resigned breath. He dealt with books and numbers and policies on a daily basis. The least he could do was look over the journals of record to ensure the castle's affairs were in as much order as possible.

"Where are Mr. Fawkes's notes?" he asked. "While I'm waiting on the aviary renovations, I might as well take a look at the accounts."

Noelle tensed as if the offer had caused offense. Nonetheless, she directed him toward low shelves at the rear of the room. The bookcase was packed with bound volumes with a year engraved on each spine. He frowned. For a short period of time around five to ten years ago, there were two journals for each year.

Curious, he collected the volumes spanning the last dozen years and carried them to his desk.

As Benjamin flipped through the books, Mr. Fawkes's hand slowly and inexorably devolved from clean and precise to an unintelligible scrawl. Numbers were no longer summed, but scribbled. Annotations as to what items were even being referenced began to appear as afterthoughts at best.

Unease churned in his stomach. This wasn't something he could resolve in an afternoon. Organizing this level of chaos, checking the facts, filling the gaps… It would take months to put to rights.

Months Benjamin did not have.

Heart heavy, he reached for the next journal.

This one was the first duplicate. He let out a deep breath before lifting the cover.

This was a different hand. Bold. Confident. Unerring. He recognized it at once. Its architect was the same woman who had just handed him a fully researched report containing every detail even peripherally related to his grandfather's aviary. His esteem rose even higher.

Noelle had done more than fill in the blanks. She had checked and cross-referenced, trimmed duplicates and made tallies. This wasn't merely a correction to Mr. Fawkes's missteps. It was a masterwork. Its information and presentation more precise and illuminating than any previous volume.

Quickly, Benjamin flipped through the remaining journals. He was not surprised to discover more of the same. Mr. Fawkes's contributions, increasingly incomprehensible. Noelle's, stunningly thorough. He was in awe of the quality. Parliament had voted acts into law that weren't half as elegant and detailed as this.

The year the duplicate journals ceased must have been the year she fully replaced her mentor. Benjamin was astonished Mr. Fawkes had managed to teach her at all with the books in such disarray. Noelle must have taught herself everything she needed to know by performing the painstaking research required to remake Mr. Fawkes's journals into something useful. Good God, she was clever.

Noelle hadn't become Grandfather's "clerk." She had become his savior, and Mr. Fawkes's as well. The counting house—and every account the castle was responsible for collecting or paying—would be in complete disarray without Noelle's timely rescue. Benjamin could not help being impressed at how smart and capable she was.

No wonder she'd had every detail about the aviary at her fingertips. It wouldn't exist without her. None of Grandfather's projects would.

Had her patrons even realized what a treasure they had? If Grandfather truly cared about his aviary, he would've put Noelle in charge. She would have had it stuffed with partridges in a trice. Two of every bird in England, no doubt.

He frowned. Why *had* Grandfather assigned the task to Benjamin, of all people? He knew the least about Cressmouth of anyone named in the will. Grandfather had to have realized Benjamin wasn't interested in the outcome. He wouldn't be bothering with the partridge and the champagne at all if the fate of his mother's locket didn't hang in the balance.

"You're scowling," Noelle said suddenly. "Do the journals not meet your approval?"

Before he could reply, the door swung open and a woman in a light blue gown and a colorful scarf rushed in.

Splendid. His muscles tensed. Instead of a duke alone in a room with one female, now there were two. He gave the new arrival a closer look. Nearing thirty years of age, at least this one did not appear to be a debutante. Perhaps Noelle had summoned a chaperone after all.

"It is adorable." The woman rushed forward to

envelop Noelle in a quick embrace before pointing both index fingers at her throat. "It's perfect."

The scarf, Benjamin realized. Noelle must have presented her friend with a scarf.

"Your Grace, I present Miss Penelope Mitchell." Noelle's laughing eyes were not on him, but her friend. "Penelope, this is His Grace, the Duke of Silkridge."

"Mr. Marlowe's grandson," she breathed, as if that were Benjamin's greatest accomplishment. "How do you do? Isn't this the cleverest scarf you ever saw?"

"It's a thoughtful gift," he teased, "but I don't know about 'clever.' There isn't a colder corner of England."

Miss Mitchell laughed. "Or a more stylish one. I have dozens of scarves. This is the first one that has been personally knitted for me by Miss Pratchett."

His gaze flew to Noelle. Her organizational skills had not only conquered accounting journals, but also colored yarn. She was not just intelligent, but *talented* as well. Full of hidden layers.

Deuce it all, Benjamin had not needed another reason to hold her in high esteem. He had found her unforgettable the last time. Fate was cruel indeed to make her all the more fascinating.

"Of course you would think Cressmouth cold," Noelle told him. "You weren't even wearing your scarf when you arrived."

"I didn't bring one," he admitted. He had not planned on staying long enough for sartorial choices to matter. One night, no complications. And now...

"Miss Pratchett could lend you one," Miss Mitchell suggested. "She has an entire armoire full of scarves she knitted herself."

Noelle's cheeks flushed pink.

"That won't be necessary," Benjamin said quickly to extricate her from obligation. The next time he braved the horrid weather, it would be to climb in his carriage and go home.

Noelle sat on the edge of her desk and faced her friend. "You did not come all the way up here to show me a scarf I knitted myself. Out with it."

"It's a new perfume," Miss Mitchell admitted. She removed a small glass vial from a leather satchel.

Noelle brought the vial to her nose and lifted the stopper. "It smells... pretty?"

"It's supposed to this time. I'm looking for people to test it." From her satchel, she pulled the smallest accordion bellows Benjamin had ever seen. "Individual drops are too inefficient a delivery method. I'm developing a new dispersal system."

"Silkridge volunteers," Noelle said without hesitation.

With a practiced motion, Miss Mitchell squeezed the bellows shut. An immediate cloud of perfume shot from the opening and enveloped Benjamin in a fog of vanilla and lilac.

He coughed into his fist and waved a white handkerchief in the air to dispel the fragrant mist surrounding him. If his gesture of surrender also dispelled the diabolical women giggling to themselves, so much the better.

Noelle stroked her chin. "I believe it's too…"

"Powerful?" Miss Mitchell guessed.

"Feminine," Noelle corrected with a laugh.

"Perfect. This version is for women. The scent is meant to arouse the passions of gentlemen." Miss Mitchell lowered her voice. "I hope the duke isn't attracted to himself all day."

"I'm sure he's used to that," Noelle promised dryly.

Benjamin glared at them both. "You're going to need a smaller bellows."

"She's a scientist, not an engineer," Noelle said. "Her perfumes sell to apothecaries by the drum."

"Although I had hoped…" Miss Mitchell gave her pocket-sized bellows a frown. "Ah, well. I suppose clients can continue applying perfume drop by drop if that's what the public wishes."

"It's a lovely scent," Noelle said firmly. "No matter how one applies it. Where are you off to now?"

"Back to the laboratory." Miss Mitchell returned her items to the leather satchel. "All that's left is proof of efficacy. A few more trials should do it."

"Be sure to come out of your workshop by tomorrow night," Noelle said. "You won't wish to miss *The Winter's Tale*."

Miss Mitchell brightened. "I would never."

"*The Winter's Tale*, the Shakespeare play?" Benjamin asked.

Noelle's eyes shone. "Mr. Fawkes adores Shakespeare. He started the tradition."

Of this, Benjamin had no doubt. "I didn't realize Cressmouth had a theater."

"No theater," Miss Mitchell explained. "At least, not the enclosed variety. We've an amphitheater on the other side of the village that we use for plays."

"Are you mad?" He stared at the women in disbelief. "You sit outside for three hours in this weather? On purpose?"

Noelle's eyes laughed at him. "I told you. It's a Christmas tradition."

"It's January," he reminded them.

"Not Christmastide," Miss Mitchell explained helpfully. "The *town* of Christmas."

"For the last time, it's not—" Benjamin gave up.

"Will you be attending?" Miss Mitchell asked him.

Benjamin gave a theatrical shudder. "Absolutely not. I want nothing to do with Christmas."

Miss Mitchell frowned. "The village or the celebration?"

Benjamin heroically refrained from pointing out that the constant confusion would end if they left the village's original name alone.

"Both," Noelle said. "He'll leave it all behind as soon as he's able."

"When he does, there will be one less duke in Christmas," Miss Mitchell said with a sigh.

Benjamin stared at her. "Not you, too."

Noelle raised her brows. "Not her, what?"

He was starting to believe the entire village had

conspired to drive him mad. "At the reading of the will, some woman claimed there were twelve dukes in Cressmouth."

Noelle exchanged glances with Miss Mitchell.

"The mathematics appear sound," her friend confirmed.

"Low, if anything." Noelle tilted her head to one side and pursed her lips as if counting mentally.

"There are not twelve dukes in Cressmouth," Benjamin burst out in annoyance.

"How would you know?" Noelle asked reasonably. "Can you even name twelve *people* in Cressmouth?"

He folded his arms over his chest. "I challenge you to name all twelve dukes, then."

"Well, there's you," Miss Mitchell began. "Obviously."

"And the Duke of Azureford," Noelle continued. "And Olive Harper's famous stallion."

"You're right," Miss Mitchell said. "Everyone says he's an excellent stud horse."

"'Duke' the stud horse?" Benjamin said in disbelief. "That's one of your dukes?"

Noelle raised her brows. "You've heard of him?"

"Everyone's heard of him," Benjamin said, exasperated. "But he's a stallion. The literal kind. You can't count a horse as a duke."

"Why not?" Noelle asked innocently. "I've certainly met dukes who are absolute beasts."

He bit back a choked laugh. The insult was not even thinly veiled.

"Thank you again, Noelle. I'm off to work on the formula." Miss Mitchell paused at the door before disappearing into the stairwell. "Don't worry, Your Grace. I'll select a more appropriate subject to test my perfumes in the future."

Surely she didn't mean that to sound so ominous.

"She's a lady perfumer?" he asked Noelle after Miss Mitchell had gone.

"She's a chemist," Noelle answered. "Who sometimes makes perfumes."

He decided against further questions. The answers were unlikely to illuminate the matter. He needed to concentrate on returning to Parliament as quickly as possible.

Benjamin fought a twinge of guilt at being away even this long. He had dedicated himself to prioritizing duty above all else, including his personal happiness. To making himself useful. To proving his life worthwhile.

If he were truly a noble man, his responsibilities to England would take priority over his mother's locket. Above family. Above sharing a madcap morning in a counting house with Noelle.

It was just this one indulgence, he reminded himself. Once the heirloom was back in his possession he would return to the House of Lords, where he was most useful. Being alone with Noelle was a temptation he could ill afford.

He stood up. But before he could leave, a new shadow fell into the counting house.

Mr. Fawkes stood in the doorway, a jovial

smile on his ruddy cheeks and the ubiquitous worsted cap clamped over his frizzy white curls.

"I knew I would find you here, my son." Mr. Fawkes beamed at Benjamin with a paternal warmth Grandfather had never shown. "I have come to help."

Benjamin loved Mr. Fawkes like a father. He wished the old man *could* help. He had admired him for so long that seeing the slow deterioration in his journals felt like a vise around his heart.

He gestured to the freshly drafted summons for the aviary workers, who at these prices would have the last details completed by the morrow. "The aviary is sorted for now, but I thank you for the offer. You are most generous."

Mr. Fawkes's jolly face crumbled in obvious disappointment. "I'm no use at all?"

Benjamin's heart twisted. "There is the matter of a partridge…"

"I know an expert on partridges," Noelle said quickly.

He doubted this. Who on earth knew an expert on partridges? Noelle had been right to redo Mr. Fawkes's books, but a man needed to feel helpful. *Order a bird* was an easy task that would ease the old clerk's mind by proving his aid undeniably useful.

Thus decided, Benjamin smiled at Mr. Fawkes. "I put you in charge of ordering the partridge."

Mr. Fawkes gave a sharp nod. "I'm not surprised. Your grandfather appreciated a bowl of hot porridge on a cold day, too."

Benjamin cleared his throat. "Not porridge. *Partridge.*"

Noelle gestured toward the ear trumpet in Mr. Fawkes's hand. The older man immediately placed it to his ear.

Benjamin shouted into the opening. "We need a partridge for the aviary."

The old clerk's frown cleared in understanding. "A partridge for the aviary."

Benjamin's tight shoulders sagged in relief. This would work after all. "Yes. A partridge for the aviary. As soon as possible."

Mr. Fawkes straightened his spine with renewed confidence. "You shall have it tomorrow, Your Grace."

He gave a merry click of his heels and marched off.

Benjamin ought to take this opportunity to do the same.

"That's dealt with," he told Noelle gruffly. "I believe I'll retire for the day. Good night."

She nodded without looking up. No doubt she was the one person in Cressmouth who wished him gone as urgently as Benjamin himself.

He carried the stack of summons downstairs to be dispatched at once, and instructed the footmen not only to wait for a reply, but to promise an even greater increase in wages if the answer was anything but yes.

With the restoration of the aviary sorted, Benjamin headed back upstairs toward his guest chamber. At the landing, he belatedly realized he had no idea where he had been transferred. Noelle had mentioned she had taken the liberty of moving him. Had it been a jest?

He caught sight of a passing maid and inquired if he had indeed been assigned to a new room.

"That you have, Your Grace." She gestured down a familiar corridor. "Last door on your left."

His breath caught. Not a guest chamber. His old room. The private quarters that had once belonged to Benjamin himself.

He thanked the maid and made his way quickly down the corridor.

When he pushed open the door, he was not greeted by cobwebs or a stuffy chill, but a bright fire and a silver tray piled with his favorite cakes. He breathed in the warm, familiar scents.

Noelle had done this, he realized. She had brought back a slice of his past and made a gift of it to him in the present. His heart thumped. She was more than a clerk or personal advisor. This move had given her away.

Whether she wished to admit it or not, a small part of her still cared.

CHAPTER 6

*N*oelle curved her fingers about the warm teacup in her hands and lowered her face to breathe in the fragrant, familiar aroma. These were her favorite moments of each morning.

Although her friends loved to tease her for her unusual taste in tea, the detour through the glasshouse to pluck fresh mint ensured she started each day with nature and beauty. Then, once she arrived at the castle's dining room, she broke her fast surrounded by hundreds of people she had known and loved her entire life.

What could be better than indulging a favorite ritual among such marvelous company? Until recently, Noelle might have answered *Nothing could be better*.

Today, the minty steam flushing her cheeks did not bring the same simple joy as usual. Instead of joining her friends and neighbors in conversation, her mind was locked on the gentleman least likely to partake of Cressmouth's many charms.

When she'd heard Mr. Marlowe's words for his grandson at the reading of the will, Noelle had fully expected a man as busy and important as the Duke of Silkridge to laugh off the preposterous terms of his bequest and return to London without any attempt to fulfill the eccentric requirements.

She knew better than to read too much into the fact that Silkridge had stayed. He was not on holiday. He had been coerced into an unexpected delay that very much went against his plans.

But what about Noelle's plans to keep her distance? She, too, had been maneuvered into deviating from her safe, comfortable routine. She had been assigned as helpmate to a man she'd never expected to lay eyes on again. But now that she had...

She set her empty cup onto its saucer and straightened her spine. Just because he was as handsome and maddening and temporary as ever did not mean she could use the dining room as her private refuge.

After all, she was not afraid of falling in love with Silkridge all over again. She knew better this time. Besides, her role as personal advisor meant that every time she helped him fulfill the terms of the will, she was also hurrying him back out of her life. Which was what she wanted. Wasn't it?

Enough stalling. Noelle prided herself on not being the sort to dither, and she wasn't about to start today.

Without further ado, she marched from the dining room to the winding stone staircase leading up to the counting house and mounted the narrowing steps with determination. She was *impervious* to the Duke of Silkridge. She would prove it.

Even before her booted feet crossed the final threshold, Noelle sensed his presence.

He was seated at the oversized mahogany desk that had once belonged to his grandfather, himself oversized in both body and spirit. Silkridge was dwarfed by neither. His presence seemed to fill the small room.

As always, everything about him was portrait-perfect. His jaw, strong and smooth. His hair, styled just so. The cut of his suit expensive, his waistcoat understated, his cravat a work of art. She swallowed.

He *looked* like a duke. One could tell at a glance. He looked as though he could rise from behind the desk and go directly to address Parliament or bow over his future duchess's hand in a London ball-room. Silkridge did not look like Cressmouth.

He looked like trouble.

There. That should put her spinning heart to rights. Noelle did her best to ignore his proximity as she crossed to her own small desk in the corner.

After taking a seat, her awkwardness did not ease. The duke, however, seemed perfectly at home in a room Noelle had come to think of as hers.

No. This would not do. If this forced together-ness reminded her of all the ways in which they were incompatible, surely politeness dictated that she should return the favor.

"Good morning," she called out cheerily. "Isn't this a lovely Christmas day?"

One could almost see his bubble of practiced calm shatter.

"It's January." He cast her a dark look over a pile of journals.

"Christmas the village," she said with an exuberant grin. "Have you ever seen a lovelier village?"

A muscle twitched at his temple. "I don't visit villages."

"Then you agree," she replied at once, her smile even bigger. "This one is the finest you've ever seen."

He was not amused. "The people here are too…"

"Happy?" she suggested helpfully. "Compassionate? Thoughtful?"

"Friendly," he concluded as if there were no greater horror in all the world. "Every one of them insists on conversing with me whenever I pass too close."

Did they? How positively delightful. This time, Noelle's grin was unfeigned.

"You're famous," she pointed out. "And you know how Christmas loves dukes."

"I can't imagine why," he gritted out. "The villagers don't inquire about London or the House of Lords. They wish to complement me on being related to my grandfather."

"He's even more famous," Noelle agreed. "Mr. Marlowe—"

"If you say 'invented Christmas...'" Silkridge interrupted in warning.

Noelle had been about to describe Mr. Marlowe's philanthropy and philosophies, but now that the duke mentioned it...

"No one claims he invented Christmas*tide*," she allowed magnanimously. "But only an imbecile could fail to see Mr. Marlowe's impact on this village. Without your grandfather, it would not be Christmas."

There. Silkridge could not argue the point without invoking the inevitable comparison to an imbecile. Besides, there was nothing to argue. The timeline was stark.

Before Mr. Marlowe's arrival, the village had been doomed. Instead, he had managed to turn it into a place of celebration. A picturesque village on a mountainside, a majestic castle, a plethora of activities, music, food, smiling faces... Cressmouth was truly the happiest place on earth.

For Noelle, anyway. Silkridge appeared unconvinced.

"Why bother?" he asked.

To her surprise, the question sounded sincere rather than sarcastic. As if he acknowledged the possibility that someone might find Cressmouth charming, even if he himself failed to see any attraction.

Noelle had no such difficulty. Without Cressmouth, her life had nothing. The castle gave her a home. Mr. Marlowe had given her hope. More than that. The counting house gave her purpose, but Christmas gave her *meaning*.

"What's not to love?" she said simply.

"All of it," Silkridge answered without hesitation. "It's cold, it's far, it's only relevant once a year..."

"Christmas lives in one's heart, not on one's calendar." She lifted her shoulders. "In my case, it lives all around me."

Nor would she change a single thing. In fact, she resented his disapproval of her village, his dismissal of their joyful way of life. No one was forcing him to paint *I love Christmas* on his top hat. If he didn't see the magic, he was welcome to leave.

"I looked at the journals," he said, changing the subject entirely.

She knew those books like she knew her town. He was right. This was a much safer topic.

"Did you have a question about the contents?" she asked.

"No questions at all," he replied. "That's what's so impressive. Every piece of information one might want is presented within its pages in a clear, easy to follow manner. If one does not wish to peruse the inflow and outflow transaction by transaction, the bold headings and concise summaries quickly communicate the state of accounts at any given moment."

Her pulse skipped. That pretty speech had sounded suspiciously like a compliment. Affirming her position as an essential part of Cressmouth. She stared back at him in silence, almost forgetting to breathe. How long had she yearned to believe it was true?

She had been left on the castle steps as a baby. No note, no explanation, no name. Although the villagers had taken her in without question, although Mr. Marlowe had been a wonderful guardian and mentor, Noelle had never forgotten that she wasn't truly one of them. She had been foisted upon them by parents willing to leave a crying infant in an abandoned basket in the snow rather than keep her. Rather than *love* her.

From the moment she could toddle, Noelle had strived to be an indispensable part of her community. Not just to be needed, to be wanted, but to ensure she would never again be left behind. To convince herself she was right where she belonged.

Whether Silkridge intended to or not, his words had just affirmed she was at least important to the counting house.

"My own man of business doesn't keep books as nice as these," he continued. "I shall have to have a stern conversation with him about increasing his standards."

Noelle blinked. Was that a hint of a smile curving at the corner the duke's lips?

"Send him here," she said when she found her voice. "I shall whip him into shape."

Yes. That was definitely a smile. "You'd more likely stuff him with biscuits and hot chocolate. He would return home the most accomplished man of business in the city, but too portly to fit through my door."

She found herself smiling back. He had deduced the culprit behind the treats in his guest chamber.

The gesture had nothing to do with her feelings toward him. She was simply treating him with the same goodwill all Cressmouth inhabitants showed one another. Nothing personal.

"Before I forget," he continued, "your report on the aviary was invaluable. Every one of the workers named in your list reported for duty this morning at dawn. With so little left to do, the final touches should be completed by tomorrow." His eyes met hers. "Thank you."

There was no reason for the sudden hollowness in her stomach.

She had *meant* to be useful. Helping people was what she did. He was grateful. Considered her capable and thorough, characteristics she strived to portray. Hastening his departure was a goal they both shared. So why did she feel like she was losing?

"It is my pleasure," she managed, despite the pit in her stomach.

Perhaps she was out of sorts because she had not anticipated being praised for her efforts. Not just because she was a female in a traditionally male role, but because she was simply doing her job. Providing assistance to Silkridge had literally been her mentor's dying wish. This was her post; balancing the accounts, her responsibility.

Yet Silkridge knew all this and complimented her anyway. He'd wanted her to know he appreciated her effort and recognized her talent.

He must be wonderful in the House of Lords,

she realized. Demanding and exacting, without question. But also encouraging and fair. As generous with *thank you* as with demands.

"The papers say you are in charge of all of Parliament's committees," she blurted. "That you practically live in the Palace of Westminster."

"It feels that way at times," he admitted. "I lead several initiatives but can neither take credit nor full responsibility. The committees work together toward a common goal. Every one of us wishes to make England a safer, healthier, more prosperous home for all its people."

Noelle was not at all convinced that every lord was like Silkridge. The fact that he guided his life by such a principle caused a crack in her armor. They were not as dissimilar as she wished to believe. She cared about others. He cared about others. They both put the community first. Hers was Cressmouth. His was all of England. He was as needed in the House of Lords as she was in this counting house.

The realization that they shared similar perspectives made her traitorous heart like him all the more. Her pulse skittered. She could not stay in this room another minute.

She leapt to her feet.

He jumped to his. "What is it?"

It was the obvious concern in his magnetic blue eyes. The way he strode toward her as if to rescue her from any evil, even the demons in her own mind. It was the familiar shape of the mouth she had once kissed and never would again. It was her erratic heart, slapping its wings against her ribs as if only by allowing it to escape could she once again fly.

"I..." The word was too soft, a breath, a plea. She knew what she wanted but dared not voice it, for fear he might give it to her.

His hand touched the side of her face. It was all she could do not to nuzzle her cheek into his palm. His hand was warm, his body too close and yet not close enough.

"I'm trying as hard as I can," he whispered huskily, "not to kiss you."

She did not move away.

Neither did he. "I beg you to slap me before I lose the battle."

She could not break away. If she lifted her hand it would be to place it against his own, or perhaps to throw herself into his arms.

This was madness. He said as much himself. Yet if he was relying on her to stop him from indulging in a kiss they both knew far too dangerous to allow...

"Help!" called a footman from the stairwell. "Miss Pratchett, come quick! It's Tiny Tim!"

She and Silkridge burst apart as if galvanized.

Noelle spun toward the open door.

Silkridge was already rushing over the threshold and down the stairs. "Where is he? His sickbed? The infirmary?"

"The menagerie," the footman responded. "He lives there."

The duke paused. "Lives there?"

"He's our Christmas goat." Noelle sidestepped

the befuddled duke to follow the footman down the stairs.

"What?" The duke called down to her. "Wait, *what?*"

She did not elucidate until they had reached the foot of the stairs.

"Your grandfather brought a pygmy goat back from Africa," she explained, "and declared—"

"That it was the town's official Christmas goat?" the duke asked in disbelief.

"—that he should be called... Tim." Noelle motioned for him to hurry. "This way to the menagerie."

The duke was perhaps understandably hesitant. "What other beasts are in the menagerie? Bruce, the puma? Horatio, the puffin?"

"Just Tim," she said as the footman swept open the door. "We didn't feel it safe to introduce other animals. Tim jumps onto everything."

"Rather, he doesn't anymore," the footman put in. "Tiny Tim arrived full of vim and vigor not a week before Mr. Marlowe took ill. At first we thought his weakened spirits were due to mourning his master."

"You thought a goat was in mourning?" Silkridge repeated, incredulous. "Over a man he'd known less than a week?"

"Mr. Marlowe had a way of getting into one's heart from the very first," the footman said staunchly.

Noelle stepped between them. "What's happening now?"

"Nothing's happening." The footman gestured

at the small, white-and-black spotted goat lying listlessly in a shadowed corner. "He's been doing this for a sennight."

The duke frowned. "Why summon Miss Pratchett? She was my grandfather's clerk, not his animal trainer."

"She was his personal advisor. One of them, anyway." The footman gave Noelle a commiserating glance. "We could have called Miss Underwood, but…"

"I understand," she assured him. This was not the moment for Virginia's eccentric aphorisms. This was the time for action.

She stared at the motionless goat.

"Has he been eating?" the duke demanded.

The footman shook his head. "Appetite is always the first to go when one suffers a depression of the spirits."

Silkridge looked as though he might throttle the man.

"Has anyone else been summoned?" she asked. "An expert on goats?"

With an exasperated sigh, the duke stalked over to where Tim lay, and placed the back of his hand to the goat's furry forehead as if checking the temperature of a child. "How much has he been drinking?"

Noelle stared at the goat dubiously. At times like this, she wouldn't mind a drink herself.

"Not a drop," the footman assured him. "Of anything. We have even been adding bits of ice to his bucket to keep the water nice and cool."

"Take it out," the duke said at once. "Goats require fresh, lukewarm water or they won't drink."

The footman turned wide eyes to Noelle. "Is that true?"

She had no idea, but it was as good a plan as any.

"His Grace has no reason to dissemble," she told the footman. "Please fetch a fresh pail of water. Mind that it is not too cool."

The footman nodded. "At once."

The moment he was gone, she turned to Silkridge. "Is it true?"

"Of course it's true," he said. "I've better things to do than invent fake facts about pygmy goats. Nonetheless, you should have the footman send for an expert."

"It sounds like you are one," she admitted. "How else would you know Tim's preferred temperature for drinking water?"

"One of my properties has goats," Silkridge said dismissively, as if every land owner exhaustively researched all flora and fauna upon his property.

No wonder he was phenomenal when it came to crafting laws. He was likely the only member of the House of Lords that truly understood whatever subject they were discussing.

The footman not only returned with a pail of fresh water, but with three more footmen all bearing the same.

Silkridge raised his brows. "What's this?"

"Wasn't certain how lukewarm 'lukewarm' ought to be," the footman admitted. "Brought four different varieties to ensure Tiny Tim received his preference."

To her surprise, Silkridge did not scoff at this notion. Instead, he knelt next to the goat and offered water from first one pail, then another, until at last Tiny Tim's parched tongue lapped up more than a few drops.

"He did it," the footman breathed. "Tim's cured!"

"I suspect it will take several days to recover from severe dehydration," said the duke. "You should send for a proper veterinarian all the same."

But he scratched behind Tiny Tim's ears, rather than leaping to his feet and dusting the goat hair from his ducal breeches.

Noelle's heart thumped. Silkridge was *soft-hearted*, of all things.

Perhaps that was why she had almost kissed him. Not because he was arrogant and bullheaded and about to disappear from her life before she would get another chance. But because he constantly surprised her with proof that he was so much *more*.

She knew not to trust romantic emotions. Being kind to a goat, being nice to her, did not mean the duke was capable of falling in love with Cressmouth or anyone in it.

Even if he could, it wouldn't be enough. Noelle was never enough. Her own parents had left her. Was it any wonder a London lord would do the same?

She knew this deep into her bones. Had sworn

to never again put herself in a position to be abandoned. The very last person she should be gazing at with calf's eyes was the Duke of Silkridge. He was destined to leave her. Danger incarnate.

And yet she couldn't look away as he held a water pail to the lips of an exhausted goat and stroked its bristly hair in comfort.

The same skills he used to command Parliament were on display before her eyes. Clever and decisive, capable and compassionate. Silkridge's ability to adapt to the moment was second to none. Anyone who chanced upon the duke engaged in such a selfless activity could be forgiven for believing him incapable of inflicting pain.

He looked up at her. "You were somehow responsible for my grandfather, Mr. Fawkes, the counting house, the castle's welcome biscuits, *and* a Christmas goat?"

"I don't mind," she stammered. "Cressmouth needs me."

It had never seemed like a lot before. Or if it had, all the better. The more the village needed her, the less likely she would find herself alone.

"You deserve a period of rest," the duke said firmly. "A holiday from this endless 'celebration.'"

She shook her head. "I would never leave Cressmouth."

He snorted. Of course he felt the opposite. He couldn't wait to leave.

His inevitable departure ought to fill her with relief, not emptiness.

She knew better than to wish he would stay. It

was impossible. He was a duke. He belonged in London. She was nobody. She belonged here.

Yet she could not help but wish she could change his mind. About Cressmouth. About Christmas. About her.

If he of all people admitted Christmas was magic, it might do more than prove her right.

It could make him want to stay.

CHAPTER 7

*B*y the third morning, the counting house was starting to feel less like a tiny chamber atop a tall, solitary tower, and more like a shared retreat high above the rest of the castle. Noelle no longer feared Silkridge might be present. She secretly hoped he was.

Her disappointment at finding the room empty was quickly eclipsed by her surprise at finding it changed.

Mr. Marlowe's side of the chamber was the same. Hers now boasted new sconces in addition to daylight from the tower window, and a cushioned chair designed for the comfort of someone of her height. The area looked positively inviting.

She stepped around her desk to the new chair and eased onto the plush cushion. Firm, but not too firm. Comfortable. Not so high that her feet could not reach the floor, not so low that the desk was out of proportion. It was perfect.

She grinned to herself as she rose to fetch the

next journal in her quest to improve each one chronologically. She was almost finished with the task. With the new chair and the sunnier lighting, it would be a joy to work in the counting house today.

As she turned from the bookshelf, the scent of mint reached her nostrils.

A footman stood in the doorway bearing a teapot, toasted bread, and cheese on a silver tray. "Shall I place this on your desk?"

She nodded in wonder. The tower was too tall for bellpulls, so Mr. Marlowe had never had one installed. As king of the castle, servants brought any repast or libation he might wish throughout the day.

As junior clerk, Noelle was expected to take her meals in the communal dining rooms with the rest of the castle.

The arrangement was more than generous. Mr. Marlowe did not charge his staff or his neighbors a penny for partaking in refreshments. It had become part of her routine. Waking at dawn, walking to the glasshouse for fresh mint, stopping by the breakfast room for a bit of toast and cheese before heading up the long winding staircase to the counting room.

She had never wanted or expected more. She was still proving herself.

Yesterday, Silkridge had casually mentioned the workers had been renovating the aviary since dawn. He had been there to oversee them. Noelle had not. Her absence had not been intentional.

With both Mr. Fawkes and Mr. Marlowe, she was used to being the first to her desk in the mornings. Silkridge's dedication was a surprise. In order to beat him to the counting house today, she had skipped her morning routine.

He had anticipated far more than her early arrival.

Instead of attempting to spoil her with plates heaping with meat and eggs and the finest tea in the kingdom, he had sent a tray bearing the items she actually preferred.

But how? She hadn't seen him in the breakfast room before. Noelle doubted herself capable of missing him. Whenever he was close, her skin tingled as if charged with electricity.

Which meant the duke had been forced to actively go find out what she might want. Perhaps he remembered her love of mint tea from their youth, but her breakfast habits had changed after becoming clerk. Silkridge hadn't relied on half-remembered memories. He had investigated to ensure he presented something she desired.

And *oh*, did she desire! A shiver tingled along her skin. Try as she might to deny it, the kiss they had almost shared, the one they had no business indulging, was all she could think about.

And now, blast him, every time she sipped her favorite tea she would think of him as well.

Just as she lifted the steaming cup, he strode through the door.

She did not tease him with *Happy Christmas*. It would break his heart to realize his many acts of kindness were very much in line with the Cress-mouth spirit.

"Good morning." The low caress of his voice heated her more than the tea in her hands.

She blushed. "Good morning."

He took his seat behind his grandfather's grand desk as if he belonged there. As if they both did.

"How goes the aviary?" she inquired.

His blue eyes lit with satisfaction. "Almost finished."

Her stomach twisted. His achievement should make her happy. Bidding him a final farewell was what she wanted. Wasn't it?

He leaned back in his chair, his manner confident. "Shan't be long now. The only missing piece is a ceremonial bird and a broken bottle of wine."

Noelle had never felt less like drinking champagne.

"Thank you for the tea," she said. "And the chair."

He shrugged this away as if such gifts were an everyday part of any man's morning routine. "You are good at your post. You might as well be comfortable while doing it."

The sentiment was bittersweet. As she was helping him leave, he was helping her stay. Nothing had changed.

"What are you working on?" he asked.

She held up one of Mr. Fawkes's old journals. "Deciphering this."

"Can I help?" Silkridge asked.

She nearly dropped the book in surprise. "There's only one left to do after this. It's the last volume on the right. You'll find fresh journals on the row beneath."

Without delay, he retrieved the old volume and its new replacement and returned to the desk to work.

Noelle watched in silence for a long moment. Soon, she couldn't keep the words back any longer. "Don't you have more important things to do?"

"Yes." His clear voice was matter-of-fact. "But all the things I should be working on are hundreds of miles away. As soon as I return home, I will devote myself to catching up on all my responsibilities. Until then, why not be of service to you? After all, it's just one more day."

Just one more day.

The words were icy balls of bitter hail, pelting into her with each cold syllable.

She tried to calm the erratic beating of her heart. Why now? Why like this?

The distance between them had been so much easier when she could despise him. Now that she knew him better, she realized she had hated a version of him that had perhaps never existed.

It wasn't that Silkridge didn't care about her. It was that he cared about everyone else more. The House of Lords. England, the collective. His duty to every one of this country's noble citizens. His responsibilities to his dukedom. Noelle could never compete with that. She was an orphan, a clerk, a nobody. Their destinies could never entwine.

But with every moment she spent with him,

the more she wished for a future she could never have.

Despite having no interest in Christmas or his grandfather's castle, Silkridge was seated behind the old man's desk performing the duties of a common clerk. Not because it would aid the castle, but because it would help *her*.

That was only the latest in a long string of surprises. From the first, Silkridge had made no disparaging comments about finding a female at the helm of the counting house. The opposite. Rather than try to talk Noelle out of her choices, he respected them. Had gone out of his way to make the small room in which she spent the majority of her time into a cozier place. He was doing his best to make her life better.

She would miss him all the worse.

Her fingers trembled as she toyed with her plume. "Do you like London?"

He looked up. "Have you ever been to the city?"

She shook her head.

"Then you don't know what you're missing. It's definitely not…" He glanced about the cold stone tower. "…*this*."

Noelle winced at the reminder that even if Silkridge weren't expected in Parliament, he still would have no interest in staying here. But even if her village was all wrong for him, she wanted him to understand why it was so special to her.

"I know you hate that Cressmouth is as far from London as possible whilst still being in England, but that's what I like about it," she said. "I live in a castle. I work on a snow-dusted mountain. I, a woman, can be a clerk."

"You say that like it's a good thing," he said drolly. "Wouldn't the social whirl of a debutante be more fun than the drudgery of a clerk?"

"I don't consider it drudgery," she explained. "I have no particular love for mathematics, but I adore putting things to rights. Creating order. Organizing people and events. It does not matter to me whether I'm arranging welcome biscuits in the common rooms or the transactions that pass through this counting house. The point is helping. I would much rather be useful than useless."

A startled laugh burst from him. "Are debutantes useless?"

"Not by choice," she said. "They certainly don't grow up to be clerks. They aren't in charge of their lives at all."

He raised his brows. "Pray tell, who is in charge of debutantes' lives?"

She could not tell whether he was mocking her or genuinely curious. Perhaps he had never considered a female perspective. Now would be a fine time to start.

"First, the wet nurse and then the governess," she said slowly. "That covers the first sixteen or so years. After the come-out, the ruling parties become the sponsor and the chaperone. Once a courtship has begun, it changes again. Only her father has the power to accept a suitor's request. And after that, her husband. The end."

He frowned. "Hardly the *end*. Any debutante

who follows that path never has to work a day in her life. Once she's secured heirs, she's free to devote herself to fashion and parties and social calls. A life of leisure, by any estimation."

Noelle ran a finger down the spines of the journals she'd worked so hard on these past four years. "Perhaps that's not what I want."

"You are opposed to a life filled with pleasures?"

"I'm opposed to an *empty* life," she clarified. "I would not wish for idleness to define me. Work and play are not mutually exclusive. I may be up here in this tower six days a week, but seven days a week, I am out and about in the village with my friends and neighbors. We are all useful. And we all like having fun."

The corner of his mouth twitched. "Fun as in the annual house party with one of your many dukes?"

She narrowed her gaze at him. That tradition had begun well after his last visit. "How do you know about the annual house party?"

She could swear his cheekbones deepened with color.

"*Cressmouth Chronicle*," he admitted.

It was her turn to burst into laughter. "You subscribe to the Cressmouth gazette?"

"Of course not," he protested quickly. "My grandfather insisted upon the quarterly journal being delivered to my home, quite against my wishes. I have never been able to cancel the subscription no matter how many letters I send."

She giggled at the thought of him responding to each circular with an angry letter for having successfully received it. "You should read the articles. They're quite dreadful."

"I know," he admitted. "Why do you think I wrote so many demands for my subscription to be annulled? Whenever the deuced rag arrived, I could not prevent myself from reading it cover to cover."

"All is well," she assured him. "I have heard there are worse guilty pleasures a gentleman could have."

"Like building places to launch dirigibles?" he said wryly. "Or stocking a menagerie with precisely one malnourished pygmy goat?"

She could just imagine the duke's incredulous expression as he read each article. "Was there no mention of Tim in the latest gazette?"

"There was no latest gazette," he said. "At first I thought delivery was a little late, then shockingly late, then began to fear my requests to cancel had been answered after all. As it happened, Grandfather had fallen ill and the quarterly fell by the wayside."

Noelle's breath caught. Silkridge was right. All the villagers' attention had been on Mr. Marlowe's rapidly worsening condition. In a matter of weeks, their founder had gone from a robust, jovial man to a resting place in the castle mausoleum. She froze.

Had anyone thought to inform his grandson? Was the only information he ever received about his own grandfather the snippets he gleaned from a nonsense quarterly journal? Worse, was the real reason Silkridge had not been present for his grandfather's final days because he had not known anything was amiss until the summons arrived for the reading of the will? Horror gripped her.

"You didn't know," she whispered.

His expression shuttered, but he did not pretend to misunderstand. "I would not have come anyway."

A week ago, she would have believed that. Today, she was not so sure. Silkridge's strong sense of duty would have won out over past slights. Mr. Marlowe had to know that. Her heart clenched.

The oversight was no accident. A man who would force the *Cressmouth Chronicle* on his grandson and mention every villager by name in his will would not have left a task as obvious as informing his grandson of his ill health to chance.

Whatever rift had come between them, she could no longer presume Silkridge shouldered the blame. If the duke had not been informed of his grandfather's condition, it was because Mr. Marlowe had planned it that way. Despite how his grandson might feel.

She swallowed. "Your grandfather should have—"

"He's gone," the duke interrupted. "Let's neither beatify nor vilify him. We know what kind of man he was."

Noelle was no longer certain she knew what kind of man Mr. Marlowe had been.

This village had been home for to her, if not from the moment of her birth than at least ever since her basket was discovered on the castle steps. Silkridge could not say the same. The town had not been a home for him any more than his own grandfather had been a parental figure. An eight-page circular four times a year was not the same as having a family.

She suddenly wished she could change that for him. Undo years of estrangement and give him not only a grandfather but an entire village. If he could understand why she felt as she did about Cressmouth, perhaps he would have learned to feel the same.

But that ship had sailed.

No. It had never existed. The past was immutable. Perhaps the duke had strong reasons not to wish to stay here in the present. She straightened her shoulders. All she could do was keep her distance. Protect her heart however she could.

Footsteps sounded on the landing.

She and Silkridge broke their silent gaze and turned their heads toward the open doorway.

"Begging your pardon, Your Grace." A footman stood at the ready. "The aviary is complete. Mr. Fawkes sent me to inform you that the item you requested has been placed inside, per your wishes."

Noelle's stomach sank. The aviary was completed; the partridge delivered. There was nothing left to detain the duke from leaving. He could be gone within the hour.

"Just a moment." Silkridge turned to Noelle, his

expression inscrutable. "Since you love to organize events, can you arrange for a bottle of champagne and as many witnesses as necessary to be present outside the aviary at noon tomorrow?"

Tomorrow. He was giving her twenty-four hours to accomplish a task that could be completed in less than one. She swallowed. Perhaps the extra day was for them.

"As you please," she said quickly. "How many witnesses? The will specified a minimum of four."

His gaze lowered for a moment before he responded. "The entire village is welcome to attend."

She glanced up sharply from the notes she was writing. "You're making the official opening something for all?"

He raised a brow. "Did you think I would not?"

"I was positive you would not," she admitted. "Your grandfather's will and testament specifically stated that you are not required to do so. You've no particular affinity for the project. I would have assumed you'd rather finish the task with as little fuss as possible in order to be on your way more swiftly."

"And you would be right," he said. "But the village would prefer to be present. The aviary does not belong to me, but to Cressmouth. Perhaps I'll even get a mention in the next circular."

The corner of his mouth gave a self-deprecating quirk.

Noelle did not smile. She couldn't. Her heart was beating too rapidly at the sweetness of the gesture. He was doing the opposite of what he wished to do for the benefit of her village. Or possibly... for her.

"Very well," Silkridge said to the footman. "That will be all."

"Wait." Noelle winced. Had she just contradicted a duke in front of a servant? She would apologize later. She put the finishing touches on the announcement she had been drafting and ran over to the footman. "Please see that this gets copied and posted throughout town by the end of the day. Put it next to the bills for tonight's play."

The footman accepted the papers and headed off with alacrity.

She glanced over her shoulder toward the duke's desk and nearly jumped out of her skin to discover he was right behind her. Her pulse quickened.

He offered her his elbow. "Shall we visit the recently renovated aviary?"

"As you wish," she stammered and somehow managed to curl her shaking fingers about his arm. She did her best to ignore how good the warm strength of his muscles felt beneath her palm.

Silkridge led her down the stairs and through the castle not as if they were en route to visit a partridge, but rather off to attend the finest ball in all the land.

Noelle could not help but wonder what it would be like if that were really true. If at the end of the stroll they did not enter an aviary, but an enormous ballroom filled with dancers and chandeliers and musicians. It would be magical.

Cressmouth had no shortage of assemblies, where someone or other would take a turn at the harpsichord, but it must be nothing like London.

Nothing like arriving on the arm of the Duke of Silkridge.

Even if it would only be for one night.

The thought caused her heart to contract. If she could have one night with him, a night of joy and love and magic where anything at all was possible, would she take it? Even if she knew it would all disappear by morning? Knowing she could have him no other way would make it very, very tempting. Who could blame her for seizing onto a moment's happiness, especially if a single moment was all she could get?

She tightened her grip on his arm and thanked the heavens that she would not be put to such a test. One stolen kiss would have to be enough.

When they reached the aviary, Mr. Fawkes stood at the entrance to greet them with flushed cheeks and the triumphant smile. "The finishing touch has just been delivered."

He swept open the door.

The aviary was as gorgeous as Noelle remembered. Tall and arching, paneled with angular glass windows that the workers had done a wonderful job of cleaning. Every surface shined to perfection.

Growing up through the earth floor were dozens of bushes and trees, selected to correspond with the various types of birds Mr. Marlowe had outlined in his notes. They had been watered and trimmed into a true sight to behold.

All that was missing was the bird.

She frowned. Although she knew the aviary contained nothing more than a single partridge, the vast space seemed inordinately quiet and still.

"Do you see it?" she whispered, searching branches for a hint of feathers.

"No. I had no idea partridges were so good at the art of disguise," the duke murmured back. He turned around. "Mr. Fawkes, where is the partridge?"

"Your Grace walked right past it," Mr. Fawkes chortled. He pointed to a small tree that had not yet been planted.

A tree containing no birds at all.

The uneasy feeling in Noelle's stomach matched the expression on Silkridge's face.

He stepped forward. "That's not a bird."

"Of course not." Mr. Fawkes puffed up his chest proudly. "It's a pear tree, just like you asked."

"Not 'pear tree.'" The duke reached for Mr. Fawkes's ear trumpet. "I said..."

Rather than place the horn to Mr. Fawkes's ear, the duke handed it back to the old clerk without another word and turned to face Noelle with a desperate expression.

"Pear trees are... tastier than porridge?" she offered weakly.

Silkridge threw up his hands in exasperation. "I shall never escape this place."

His words were a knife in her gut. The duke might want to kiss her, but he didn't want to stay.

"Is something wrong?" Mr. Fawkes asked nervously.

"Thank you for your service," Silkridge

shouted into the old clerk's ear trumpet. "The castle wouldn't be the same without you."

Mr. Fawkes beamed at the duke and patted him on the shoulder. "Anytime you need me, lad. I am at your beck and call."

The duke managed to wait until Mr. Fawkes exited the aviary before letting out a long slow breath.

Noelle felt for him. The old clerk's ruined hearing had failed the duke not once but twice. Both times, Silkridge had been a remarkably good sport. She doubted his grandfather would have handled the situation with such grace. Silkridge was a good man.

She, on the other hand, was far less noble. A tiny part of her was glad that Mr. Fawkes had failed to come up with the goods as promised. His mistake had given her a reprieve from the duke's inevitable departure. She could keep him a little while longer. This was a blessing.

The duke swung his frustrated gaze from the pear tree to her. "Stop the announcements before they're posted. We will have to cancel the christening."

"Or," she said gently. "You could let me deal with this."

He stared glumly at the spindly branches devoid of fruit before him. "By tomorrow?"

Her stomach twisted. She might have considered the mix-up a dream come true, but to Silkridge it was a nightmare. He would rather be anywhere else but Cressmouth. He would leave within the hour if he could. She would do well not to forget that.

"I told you," she reminded him. "I know an expert on partridges."

He slid her a look out of the corner of his eye. "Why would any village have an expert on partridges?"

"Bird expert," Noelle amended. "Virginia loves animals. She can solve this puzzle."

"Can she?" His voice was doubtful. "Doesn't her cat love birds?"

"Not one whit," Noelle answered with forced cheer. "Don't worry. Virginia keeps everything in its place. She'll know right where to find a spare partridge."

He nodded. "Thank you."

Noelle could not quite bring herself to say *it's my pleasure*. She was ushering Silkridge out the door when all she wanted was for him to stay.

For the first time in her life, she wished she weren't so deuced efficient.

"This is our last night," the duke said as if reading her mind.

She swallowed. "Yes."

He nodded slowly. "Then I accept your help under one condition."

She frowned. Surely he wouldn't ask her to move the event up even sooner. "What condition?"

His voice grew husky. "Allow me to escort you to tonight's play."

She stared at him, her voice faint even to her own ears. "Tonight's play?"

"*The Winter's Tale*," he said. "Didn't you say it was your favorite?"

"I said it was in an amphitheater," she reminded him. "The outdoor kind."

"It will be worth it," he said softly, his blue eyes locked on hers.

Her heart leapt. Perhaps he was changing his mind about her. Perhaps she could even change his mind about Cressmouth.

"On one condition," she said, and bit her lip.

His eyebrows shot up. "Name it."

"Let me give you a tour of the village first," she said impulsively. "Show you everything the *Cressmouth Chronicle* cannot begin to cover."

He glanced over his shoulder as the wind whistled against the aviary's many panes of glass. "At this very moment?"

"One couldn't ask for a bluer sky," she said. "We can take a picnic lunch. Fruit and meats and cheeses."

His expression was skeptical. "A picnic lunch in the back of a carriage?"

"In the back of a sleigh," she corrected. "Cressmouth is made for traveling thus. Besides, how can you see the town if you keep yourself sequestered inside somewhere?"

His gaze was unreadable. She had asked for too much. He was going to say no.

"I hope it's a sleigh with a roof," he muttered.

"No roof," she chirped. "I need to fetch my coat from my chamber."

He proffered his elbow. "Shall I summon a maid?"

"No," she said quickly. "It's faster if I do it myself."

He led her toward the stairs. "Then I shall do the same. My room is down the corridor."

She knew. It was all she could think about. But how did *he* know? Her heart pumped faster. Did he lie awake at night thinking of her doing the same at the other end of the corridor?

"I won't be but a moment," he promised as he left her by her door to go and fetch his own great coat and top hat.

She hurried into her room and slid on her warmest pelisse, her kid gloves, her prettiest scarf, her thickest muff, her winter bonnet. After a moment's hesitation, she also retrieved a second scarf. One she had just finished last evening.

When she stepped out in the hall, the duke was already outside her door. She waited until they were outside in the back of the horse-drawn sleigh with a picnic basket between them before handing him the scarf.

"Put this on," she ordered. "Cressmouth won't seem nearly as cold if you are properly dressed."

"It never seems cold when I'm near you," he replied softly.

The back of her neck heated with pleasure.

He wound the scarf about his neck and opened the picnic basket. "Tell me absolutely everything about this ghastly village while I gorge myself on fruit and cheese and pretend that I'm listening."

She looked over at him sharply, but his eyes were full of laughter.

"Beast," she chastised him. She motioned for the driver to begin a sedate pace.

She and Silkridge enjoyed a leisurely picnic as they traveled through the snow-covered streets. The sky was clear, the breeze pleasantly crisp. It was a glorious Cressmouth winter day, perfect for snuggling. Thank heavens there was a picnic basket between them.

Laughing with Silkridge in the back of a sleigh was far more perilous than Noelle had anticipated. She had cared for him once before. Her heart remembered the sensation like putting on warm woolen mittens. If she did not guard herself…

"And there's the smithy," she announced breathlessly, forcing herself to concentrate on the promised tour and not to give over to emotion. "The French family who owns it knows everything about blacksmithing and carriages. The Duke of Azureford swears by their craftsmanship."

"He would," Silkridge said. "Azureford is always nattering on about winning phaeton races."

Noelle grinned as they rounded another corner. "All this open land belongs to Olive Harper, who breeds racehorses. She has several phenomenal stallions absolutely everyone is after, and won't sell no matter how high an offer she receives."

"I know," Silkridge said. "Her family's stud farm is infamous throughout England. If I have to sit through one more aside in the House of Lords for peers of the realm to discuss horseflesh instead of policy…"

"Do you want to listen to the tour or to give

it?" she teased him. But she enjoyed hearing stories about Cressmouth's influence on London, rather than the other way around.

He waved his hand. "Continue, continue."

Over the next hour and a half, she managed to point out the majority of the town's sights and people. That was, between nibbles of food, and giggles at the duke's constant interruptions.

Everyone they passed called out cheery greetings, and although the duke made certain to mutter *humbug* under his breath each time, Noelle was increasingly convinced he did so for her benefit rather than his.

By the time they arrived at the amphitheater, being with him felt as natural as the afternoon sun. When they took a seat near the center facing the stage, it was all she could do not to nestle her head on his shoulder and curl into his warmth.

The heated glances he had been sending when he thought she didn't notice indicated he was feeling much the same.

"Is being a counting house clerk what you want from your life?" he asked suddenly, his eyes searching.

"I'm good at it," she said simply. "It's important."

"To you or to Cressmouth?" he asked.

She frowned. "It's the same thing."

"It is not the same." His expression was intense. "You should not concentrate on Cressmouth to the exclusion of your own life."

"I don't mind," she assured him. Cressmouth was her family, her home. She wouldn't abandon their needs in favor of her own. "I don't need both."

The duke's gaze did not waver. "I think you should be able to have it all."

He made her *want* it all.

In that moment, Noelle realized the horrible truth. It was too late for shields. Allowing him back into her heart wasn't the problem.

He had never left.

CHAPTER 8

$\mathcal{A}$ fortnight ago, Benjamin would have laughed at anyone who suggested he would one day voluntarily spend several hours outside in the winter cold away from all his responsibilities, away from London. Even this afternoon when he had offered to escort Noelle to the play, he hadn't known it would become one of the most enjoyable days of his life.

How he wished he could wrap his arm about her and pull her close. Unfortunately, just like the ride in the open sleigh, they were much too visible.

Although they had arrived at the amphitheater an hour early, eager spectators had already begun to fill the long, curved rows. Snow had been cleared from the stone benches and the sky was a brilliant blue. He could not deny it. If one were to be forced to watch an outdoor play, in the middle of winter, one could not ask for finer weather.

The breeze had given Noelle's cheeks a rosy glow. Despite the protective barrier of a winter bonnet, a few golden tendrils had managed to come loose and bounced becomingly against the side of her face.

He forced himself to tear his gaze from her beautiful profile before he gave himself away. The amphitheater was growing full.

The couples amongst the audience were easy to spot. The touch of a hand, an intimate glance, two bodies seated so close as to become one. His chest tightened.

Once upon a time, Benjamin would have scoffed at romantical fancy. That way lay inevitable sadness. He was too strong to be taken by such a naive emotion. His heart, too well protected.

But now when he glimpsed couples in love, he no longer experienced a sense of satisfaction at having managed to keep such ill-fated folly from his life. Instead, a strange loneliness entered his chest. A yearning to expand his heart rather than hide it. If only for a moment.

He brushed the back of Noelle's fingers with his own. "Thank you for letting me borrow a scarf," he murmured.

She gave a quick shake of her head. "It's yours."

And there was that melancholy again. Hope warring with emptiness. He shook his head. "I shall not rob a lady of her scarf."

"It's not mine," she said shyly. "I made it for you."

Those five words warmed him all the way to his heart.

Even though he had hurt her once before, even

though he could not stay, she had still knitted him something to keep him warm. It worked. With her, he felt invincible.

He couldn't recall the last time anyone had done something just because they thought he would like it. Not until her. She had managed to do something thoughtful every day. Starting with arranging for him to have his old bedchamber back.

They now slept on the same floor. In the same wing. Down the same corridor. His blood heated. Perhaps *slept* was too ambitious a word. He had barely caught any rest at all from lying awake each night thinking about her.

She smiled up at him from beneath her bonnet. "Thank you for agreeing to a sleigh ride."

Absolutely his pleasure. "I cannot imagine a better tour guide."

"Did you like the village a little better than you imagined?"

"It isn't terrible," he admitted. "Given its unfortunate location."

"High praise," she said, her eyes twinkling. "Perhaps you should become a Cressmouth tour guide yourself."

Of course she was teasing. He was the last man for the job. Noelle, on the other hand, was perfect here. Everyone they passed clearly adored her. And why wouldn't they? She was selfless and friendly, cheerful and outgoing...

Benjamin's complete opposite.

"You're not coming back, are you?" she asked, her voice quiet. "When you leave."

He shook his head. "I have no family here. Why do *you* stay?"

"Because I do have family here," she gestured around the crowded amphitheater. "Everyone you see is my family."

"You know what I mean."

"I don't think you know what I mean," she returned, her dark gaze intense. "Family isn't limited to blood. It's who you make it. Family is a *choice*." Her voice cracked. "*Home* is a choice."

"I am sure this village is perfect for those who have chosen to make it their home," he admitted grudgingly. "I cannot be one of them. I am needed in the House of Lords and on my own properties. The aviary needs to open as soon as possible."

"We have an appointment with the expert on partridges in the morning," she said, her eyes on the empty stage rather than on him. "Will you be leaving as soon as the bottle breaks?"

He swallowed the words he wished he could say and forced himself to be practical. "Almost. I'm not leaving without my mother's locket."

Her gaze snapped to his. "It is very important?"

"The most important thing in my life." He cleared his throat. "Next to my country, of course."

"Of course," she murmured.

But he didn't expect her to understand. Noelle still believed his grandfather a maker of miracles, not a breaker of dreams. She didn't know the whole truth.

Benjamin wasn't even convinced playing the fool's game with the wine and the partridge would result in success. For all he knew, Grandfather might have been buried with the locket. If only the solicitor had been willing to tell Benjamin where to find it! Just to prove to himself that he wasn't fighting for nothing. That all his years of anger and hurt and waiting had not been in vain.

Noelle's voice softened. "What's wrong?"

An idea caught him. His heart raced. In this town, Noelle knew everything and everyone. She had perhaps entered the fee for guarding the locket into one of her journals.

His words tumbled out faster than he meant. "Do you know where the items inventoried as part of my grandfather's estate are deposited?"

"Your locket, specifically?" she asked.

"*My* locket, specifically," he agreed with more emotion than he intended.

She nodded. "All jewelry is being held by Angelica Parker."

Of course. The artist of the jewel-encrusted tiaras. Thanks to the tour he just witnessed, Benjamin knew exactly where to find her.

It was all he could do not to leap up from the stone bench, tear off through the crowd, and keep running until he arrived out of breath at the jeweler's door. He needed to see the locket. To ensure it still existed, to verify the condition it had been kept in, to feast his eyes on the beloved portrait.

He forced himself to remain seated. Not for the impending play or even the scandal such a departure would cause, but for Noelle. This play meant something special to her. He wanted this evening to be special for both of them.

It was all they would have. He would not ruin it.

"Silkridge, as I live and breathe!" shouted a jolly male voice from right behind him.

Benjamin twisted in his seat and stared in disbelief at two dapper London gentlemen that looked for all the world as if they had been dropped into the most delightful soirée they'd ever seen.

"Do you know them?" Noelle whispered.

Did he ever. They were his heirs presumptive. First cousins with no courtesy title and nothing but free time.

"Miss Pratchett, may I introduce Nicholas and Christopher Pringle. Cousins, this is Miss Pratchett."

"You must call me Christopher," his younger cousin said without hesitation. "Two Mr. Pringles are impossible to remember."

"I can be memorable," said his elder cousin with a wolfish smile. "Some call me Saint Nicholas."

"Because he is absolutely wicked," Christopher stage-whispered. "Don't worry, my dear. You are safe with me."

"She is safer with *me*," Benjamin said, more forcefully than he had intended. "Why are you here?"

Before the words were out of Benjamin's mouth, Nicholas had already been distracted by a pretty face across the crowd and took off in immediate pursuit.

Christopher sat down next to him with a wide

smile. "Once we heard you were here, we had to see for ourselves. I can't recall the last time you took a holiday." He winked at Noelle. "Although, now I understand the attraction."

"Miss Pratchett lives here in Cressmouth and has been kind enough to show me her village," Benjamin said quickly. He did not want to imply that there was any more to it than that. There could never *be* anything more to it than that. Best to change the subject. "I cannot believe you followed me here. I did not mean to encourage a trend."

"Don't worry," Christopher assured him. "It was a trend long before your visit. Did you know the Duke of Azureford has a home here?"

"It's been mentioned," Benjamin said with a sigh.

"It's delightful," Christopher said, glancing about in obvious pleasure. "I have never seen such a charming place in all my life. Who wouldn't wish for Christmastide year-round? I could live here forever."

"It's not—" Benjamin began, but Christopher was already off and running, bubbling over with all the wonderful ways Cressmouth was superior to any other village he had ever seen.

"*He* should be the tour guide," Noelle whispered in Benjamin's ear.

He sighed. Men like his cousins flocked here for a distraction, which was a luxury Benjamin could not afford. He ought to concentrate on his responsibilities. Return to the real world.

"No wonder it is now such a point of pride to

have a cottage in Christmas," Christopher was saying. "I've been here all of two hours and I vow I've made a hundred friends for life. Have you ever been so charmed, Silkridge?"

Benjamin tightened his jaw. "It's not called—"

"Maybe I should stay," Christopher said suddenly. "Or at least take an annual holiday here. Is that a strange thing to do?"

Noelle answered before Benjamin could. "Many have dual residences. Anyone with a title, of course, and several others who have family elsewhere but also consider us their home. I am not at all surprised you've made fast friends of my neighbors. That's the Christmas spirit."

"I like that," Christopher exclaimed. "I shall work on my Christmas spirit."

Benjamin heroically refrained from dropping his face into his palm.

Before his eyes, Noelle and his cousin engaged each other in an animated conversation about all the wintry fun that could be had within the village walls. Sledding, wassailing, roasting chestnuts on an open fire.

If they noticed Benjamin sitting stoically between them, they gave no sign. It was what he deserved, he supposed. His retribution for lack of Christmas spirit. Or punishment for his intense desire to keep all other men away from Noelle.

As much as he longed to sweep her into his arms and carry her out of this amphitheater into the first private corner where they could be alone, he recognized such thoughts for the fantasy they were. A woman like her would not seek his money or title, but his entire heart. She wouldn't settle for a compromise. She would expect him to make room in his priorities for a holiday he had sworn off entirely. She wouldn't increase his solitary family by one but rather by an entire village.

Noelle would never leave Cressmouth. It would be like ripping her heart from her body. And he could not stay. Every mention of Christmas was a knife through his chest, a constant reminder of all that he had lost, the pain that he had been through, the suffering his grandfather inflicted even now.

This village would never be his home. It was a living nightmare.

"What is the most famous aspect about Cressmouth?" Christopher asked. "Has it a particular claim to fame?"

Noelle thought it over. "I suppose the twelve Dukes of Christmas."

Benjamin could not stay silent anymore. "Horses do not count. There are currently thirty odd dukes in all of England. I cannot possibly believe that a third of them choose to holiday in this ice house."

"You're the odd one," Christopher said with a laugh.

Noelle nodded up at him solemnly. "Christmas is for believing."

"It's not called—" Benjamin burst out laughing despite himself. "You're doing it on purpose now, aren't you?"

"I cannot imagine what you mean." She blinked

at him innocently. "I must say your cousin is quite charming."

Yes, Benjamin supposed he was.

If coming face-to-face with Noelle after all these years had reminded Benjamin of Christmases past, then Christopher was the very embodiment of present-day Christmas.

It was more than a matter of living in the moment. It was as though Christopher was living the life Benjamin would be living if he had made different choices. Christopher was gregarious and easy-going. As comfortable in small gatherings as in a crowd. He loved bobbing for apples and singing carols and he likely wouldn't leave Cressmouth without purchasing a sleigh. He was carefree in a way that Benjamin never had been, even as a child. How could he be?

Benjamin's life had begun with tragedy. His mother had not died during childbirth, but rather from complications that had plagued her thereafter. She lived just long enough to pose for a miniature portrait with him in her arms, and then was taken from him. Taken from them all.

Grandfather had blamed Benjamin ever since.

Father had been his only ally, but he too had been ripped from Benjamin before his time. When Grandfather stole the locket, withheld the last link to family…

If it had not been for those formative events, would Benjamin be like Christopher today? Might he be cheerfully milling through a crowd of strangers, turning them into lifelong friends one by one?

He was jealous, he realized in surprise. Not of his cousin's carefree life, but of his easy connection with the villagers. Over the last few days, he had realized that the people of Cressmouth weren't being so nice and solicitous to him because of his title, or even his connection to the village's founder.

They were just *nice*.

Benjamin hadn't been experiencing the spirit of Christmas. He was experiencing the spirit of *Cressmouth*.

The villagers had become more important to Benjamin than any other shire in England, perhaps because they weren't nameless and faceless like the rest of the population. He no longer cared about their welfare on a policy level, but a personal one.

"Wherein our entertainment shall shame us, we will be justified in our loves," shouted an actor. "For indeed…"

The Winter's Tale had finally begun. Unlike the good people of Cressmouth, Benjamin had not seen this play before. Or any play, to be honest. He kept himself far too busy. Although he could not imagine sitting through the exact same play year after year, the audience was rapt with attention.

He leaned back slightly for a better view. He was watching Noelle rather than the play. He couldn't help it. She was far more interesting and a lot less to read. Every time he looked at her, his thoughts jumbled. He wished he had kissed her. He was relieved he had not. All his thoughts of her were contradictions. She made him want to stay. She made him want to flee. She made him... *want*.

His arms felt empty without her in them. He yearned to know what it might be like to wrap them about her, to feel her body pressed against his. To claim her mouth with a kiss.

Only her mouth, of course. He could claim nothing else, and he should not even be thinking of that much. It did not matter that she consumed his every thought, his every desire. It did not matter that she somehow made him feel at home no matter whether they found themselves in an amphitheater, on a sleigh, in a counting house, an aviary staring at a pear tree.

No matter how fond he might be of Noelle, she was not of his status. He could not have her. She was his grandfather's clerk. This was not his home. He had to try to remember.

"My prettiest Perdita!" called Prince Florizel from onstage. "But, oh, the thorns we stand upon..."

Noelle's breath caught.

He touched his fingers to hers in question.

"Prince Florizel allows nothing to stand in his way," she whispered, her eyes shining as she gazed down at the stage.

The pieces clicked together. Although Perdita was abandoned as a baby, Florizel fell in love with her anyway. *Chose* her anyway. No wonder Noelle loved this part. Benjamin's chest clenched in regret.

He could not be her Prince Florizel. There was

no magic spell to save them in the end. No running off to Sicily together.

Regardless of any wild fancies in Benjamin's heart, he was not in a position to take a wife outside his class. Not when thumbing his nose at Society's conventions could lose him political allies and impede his ability to make a difference in the House of Lords. Too many people were counting on him.

"Sure the gods do this year connive at us," said Autolycus on stage, "and we may do anything..."

Benjamin understood the sentiment. He knew all too well what it was like to feel as though the fates had conspired against him. Being with Noelle made him wish he *could* do anything. Watching her laugh at lines she had heard countless times and tear up at melodrama she already knew would occur was the most endearing thing he had ever seen.

She was not tired of this place, this play, this eternal Christmastide. She loved it. She looked forward to every aspect with anticipation and allowed herself to feel it all so deeply it was as if every line were experienced anew.

For so long, Benjamin had wondered why a woman as intelligent as Noelle wasn't more like him, and now he could not help but wonder the opposite. While he could not foresee any future for himself that did not involve utmost dedication to duty and responsibility, he was intensely grateful she had been spared the same fate.

The pleasure she took from life was infectious. She was a force impossible to deny. He had visited the bedside of a goat, for God's sake. Was willingly sitting in the open air in the middle of the winter with a warm woolen scarf wrapped tight about his neck. A scarf Noelle had knitted for him, not knowing if she would ever witness him using it.

"I am ashamed," said Leontes onstage. "Does not the stone rebuke me, for being more stone than it?"

Benjamin was glad they had spent time together outside the counting house. The sleigh, the picnic, the play. He could not recall a happier day. She could even make a snowy evening seem warm and inviting. He would remember this forever.

He tried not to think about the moment he would have to say goodbye. Surely she understood why he couldn't stay. He did not choose to be a duke, to have a seat in the House of Lords, but it was not a responsibility one could shirk.

His throat tightened as he realized he hoped for her approbation. Her acknowledgment that he had no choice, that of course England must be his priority in all things, would perhaps ease the pain of having to walk away.

"Oh, peace, Paulina! Thou shouldst a husband take by my consent," said Leontes onstage. "This is your son-in-law, and son unto the king, who, heavens directing, is troth-plight to your daughter. Hastily lead away."

The audience erupted into applause.

Benjamin blinked. It was over?

He got to his feet with the others, unable to believe he had spent the entire play casting surreptitious glances at Noelle.

Her friends suddenly surrounded them.

"That was wonderful," exclaimed one. "I love it when the bear chases Antigonus off the stage."

"The best year yet," Noelle agreed with a smile. She glanced up at Benjamin. "Did you enjoy the evening?"

"Even more than I anticipated," he admitted.

"Let's go caroling," bubbled another of Noelle's friends. "It's a Christmas tradition!"

Benjamin had no idea if "Christmas" in this case referred to the incorrect name of the place or the festive period that had passed over a month ago, but he couldn't summon the urge to correct them. It was their village. They could do as they liked. He wouldn't spoil their fun.

But he couldn't join them.

Noelle smiled up at him, her eyes sparkling. "Do say you'll come. Carols are ever so much jollier after a bowl or two of mulled wine."

Looking at her, he was tempted. She lived and loved so openly and freely. Who wouldn't wish to share in her joy?

"I can't," he said honestly. This was his opportunity to visit the jeweler holding his mother's locket and find out what condition it was in. "Do have fun with your friends. Where shall I meet you tomorrow?"

"How about half ten, in the glasshouse? I am meeting Miss Mitchell to give my opinion on her newest scent."

He narrowed his eyes. "You don't mean to ambush me with perfume again, do you?"

"One must take risks," she admonished him with a twinkle in her eye.

"I shall take that under advisement," he said gravely.

Before her friends could renew their efforts to include him in their fun, he edged away from the crowd and picked his way down the snow-packed lanes toward the jeweler's shop.

His heart beat faster and faster in trepidation the closer he came to the jeweler. It was a moment of truth. Either Grandfather had finally been true to his word, or the old man had taken the locket to his grave.

Hands shaking, he rapped upon the jeweler's door.

No answer came. His frenzied knocks received no answer.

The play. Of course. He clenched his chapped fists in frustration. The entire village had filled the amphitheater. Perhaps even now, the jeweler was off wassailing and would not return for hours.

He stared doubtfully at the rustic cottage. It was clear that the jeweler worked on one side of the building and lived on the other. Less clear was whether finding a duke encamped upon her front doorstep would be enough to convince her to answer his questions.

He might have to wait until morning. His shoulders sagged. What was one more sleepless night?

Just as he turned to go, a pink-cheeked woman with a brisk step turned onto the front path.

His heart thumped. "Miss Parker, my apologies for calling so late and unannounced."

"I am never too busy for a social call," she said cheerfully. "And the sun has not fully set. May I invite you in for a cup of tea, Your Grace?"

He cleared his throat. "I'm afraid this is not a social call."

She tossed a merry look over her shoulder as she unlocked the door. "Is Your Grace in the market for a tiara?"

"Tiaras tend to clash with my hats," he said solemnly. "Else I would be your best customer."

"I shall design one to fit your top hat," she replied with a glint in her eyes so wicked he feared her words were true.

"I've come about my mother's locket," he said quickly. "The heirloom mentioned in my grandfather's will. I have been told you are the keeper of all named jewelry."

"Indeed." She beckoned him inside and into an impressive workman's chamber, with all manner of tools hanging from the walls and behind the counters.

"Do you mind showing me the locket?" he asked, hoping years of rage and hope and grief didn't appear on his face.

She hesitated. "I cannot let you take it."

"I won't," he promised. "I am a man of my word and I will fulfill my grandfather's wishes, no matter what I think of them. I want to confirm that his word is just as trustworthy. I have not seen the locket in five years. I need to ensure it is indeed the one I am after."

"Very well." From about her neck, she lifted a long chain bearing an intricate key. "If Your Grace would give me a moment?"

He nodded jerkily. He was so close now. Another moment was nothing. Soon he would know the truth.

She stepped into an adjoining room and out of sight. "Will you be in Cressmouth long?"

"I'm not here on holiday," he said, his voice as light as he could muster. "I will stay only as long as it takes to retrieve that locket."

Muffled sounds came from the other room. His heart pounded. She must be opening the safe.

"Are you looking forward to the christening party for the aviary?"

"I won't be attending." He tried not to grit his teeth. Being forced to make small talk was excruciating. He just needed to see his mother's face. "Cressmouth will have to celebrate without me."

She emerged from the adjoining room with an expression of surprise. "You're leaving immediately after tomorrow's ceremony?"

"I shall pick up the locket, jump into my carriage, and never look back." The words were brutally honest.

Retrieving the locket and escaping Cressmouth, Christmas, and his grandfather's clutches for good had always been the plan. That single-minded goal had consumed him since the day his grandfather had first stolen the locket.

Yet the idea of never seeing Noelle again suddenly made his chest feel hollow.

Without further questions, the jeweler held out her palm. "Is this the one?"

Heat stung the back of Benjamin's eyes. It *was* the locket. Exactly as he remembered it. A perfect oval, trimmed in gold lace and embossed on the front with the silhouette of an angel.

He reached for it with trembling fingers.

"May I?" The words came out too scratchy to be understood, but the jeweler nodded anyway.

He lifted the small oval in his hands. It felt weightless. Empty. As if it no longer contained his mother's soul. The gold chain dangled through his fingers, brushing between them like a strand of hair. Not that he remembered what his mother's hair had been like. All he had was the image on the inside of this locket.

If it was still there.

He undid the clasp with reverence and eased open the locket. On the left side was nothing. That space had been reserved for a future portrait that had never come to pass.

On the right side was his mother. His heart thumped in relief, and grief, and sorrow.

There she was. Smiling. Happy. Gazing at the baby in her arms with an expression of such love it took Benjamin's breath away. This was his mother. All that was left of her.

"Is it as Your Grace remembered?" the jeweler asked softly.

He feared his throat too tight for words, so he gave a short nod instead.

"These last few years, Mr. Marlowe never let it

out of his sight," the jeweler murmured. "He said it was the last portrait of his daughter."

Fury, hot and sharp, bubbled inside him. "It was the only likeness of her I ever had."

Grandfather's constant refusal to return the heirloom had been like being denied his family all over again.

Why could they not have shared her? Benjamin had offered to compromise. It would have cost so little to commission an artist to create a copy of the portrait. Grandfather had dismissed the plea out of hand. Once he'd gained possession of the locket, he'd ceased acknowledging Benjamin altogether. His fingers shook at the injustice and rejection. Why did he have to lose so that his grandfather could win? Why could they not have been family to each other?

His vision blurred as he gazed down at his smiling mother. She had loved him, his father had loved him, unconditionally, then they'd been stolen first by God and then by a grandfather who loved to *play* God with others.

Love was dangerous. It was out of one's control. The more one cared about another person the more likely they were to be ripped from one's side. The only way to protect himself from hurt was to concentrate on the things he could control. Leave Cressmouth. Encase himself in ice. Dedicate himself to his country, not love.

There was no need to fear the title dying out. Thanks to his cousins, he already had two heirs presumptive. If he kept his mind on nothing but

Parliament, there would be no need to fear anything at all.

Love only led to hurt. The only way to ensure he would never again lose someone he cared about was to do his best not to care.

"If you're satisfied..." The jeweler held out her hand.

His heart clenched. He was not satisfied. He wanted things he could not have. He wanted the emptiness inside to go away.

But he forced himself to hand back the locket. "How soon after the ceremony may I have it?"

"Immediately after the bottle breaks," she said. "Shall I prepare a cushioned jewelry box for travelling?"

Benjamin shook his head. "I'll wear it home."

He was never losing contact with his family again.

CHAPTER 9

*B*enjamin awoke long before dawn. Confirming the locket's existence had only caused the hours to stretch out that much longer. This was his last day in Cressmouth. His last day with Noelle.

His appointment with her wasn't for two more hours. He'd broken his fast, dashed off a handful of letters and responses, and was now far too restless to stay cooped up in his old bedchamber. A place he would be leaving behind for good this time.

Perhaps one last walk about the castle would put the strange sensation in his chest to rest.

He stepped out into the corridor just in time to glimpse his cousin Nicholas arriving at the landing.

Nicholas leaned against the balustrade and waited for Benjamin to approach.

"So that's where they stuffed you," Nicholas said. He gestured down the opposite corridor.

"Mine's that way. Stunning view from the mountaintop. Have you seen the horizon at dawn?"

Benjamin lifted his brows. "You are just getting back to the castle?"

"I'm just returning to my guest chamber," Nicholas clarified with a wicked smile.

"'Saint Nick,'" Benjamin muttered. "A rake to the core."

Nicholas's smile only widened. "It may be cold outside, but inside…"

"No wonder you're enamored with Cressmouth," Benjamin said.

"It has many, many charms," Nicholas assured him. "I see why so many come here for distraction."

"I don't think 'Christmas spirit' means seducing pretty maidens," Benjamin said dryly.

"I have never seduced a maiden," Nicholas said, his expression hurt. "I allow myself to be seduced by those who aren't maidenly in the least. They know exactly what they're getting. That's why they want me."

Benjamin raised a brow. "One night to slake their lust?"

"Mutual slaking," Nicholas agreed. "A rakish gentleman simply provides requested entertainment. A pleasurable evening for both parties without any promises or strings. Everybody wins."

"Perhaps that's true if no strings and no promises are indeed what both parties are after," Benjamin agreed. "I should expect it gets complicated when one party wants more than the other."

Nicholas shook his head. "That is the easiest situation to resolve. Stay away from those who want more than your body or more than one night."

"Easy," Benjamin echoed. He had spent a lifetime doing just that. "But doesn't it get... lonely?"

A dark shadow flickered across the blue of Nicholas's eyes, and just as quickly it was gone. "It's impossible to be lonely when there's always someone new to meet."

Benjamin stared at his cousin as if seeing a ghost. He had always considered Saint Nicholas his opposite in all things. It was disconcerting to have to revise that opinion.

Although the two lived unquestionably different lives, the consequence was the same. Each morning, they woke up alone. There was no one there who had shared dreams and hurts, who had been by one's side for months or years or decades. No one who could answer *yes* to *remember the time when?* No one whose touch was familiar, whose kiss felt like coming home.

Although Nicholas had chosen a different route, Benjamin now suspected they were both on the path to a very lonely future. If something didn't change, his future Christmases would be as empty as all the rest. He frowned.

Wasn't that what he wanted? He couldn't get hurt if he didn't open himself up to love.

Nick clapped him on the shoulder. "I'm off to my chamber. Where are you heading?"

"Menagerie," Benjamin answered. "I want to visit a goat."

"I've changed my mind. I'm coming with you,"

Nicholas said immediately. "I had no idea there was a goat."

When they entered the menagerie, a footman was keeping an eye over the invalid.

Benjamin hurried closer. "How's Tiny Tim?"

"Tiny Tim?" Nicholas asked.

Benjamin gestured. "Pygmy goat."

Nicholas nodded. "I see."

"Much improved, Your Grace," the footman said with obvious relief. "We are ever so grateful."

"Grateful to Silkridge?" Nicholas asked. "Did you bring the castle a pygmy goat as some sort of Christmas gift?"

"I did not," Benjamin replied. "I have made a personal resolution to deliver fewer goats as gifts this season."

"His Grace's knowledge about the beast's constitution brought Tiny Tim back from the brink of death," the footman said proudly. "It was nothing short of a miracle."

"Silkridge performed a Christmas miracle," Nicholas repeated, his expression baffled. "*You?*"

"I may have relayed a few suggestions based on my research into caprine physiology due to the livestock present on my own properties," Benjamin said humbly.

"And His Grace summoned his personal physician all the way from London," the footman continued with pride.

Nicholas blinked slowly. "You summoned your personal physician for a goat?"

"It's not just any goat," said the footman. "It's Tiny Tim."

Nicholas stared at Benjamin in disbelief.

"Not *my* physician," he explained. "A veterinarian."

Slowly, Nicholas shook his head. "You're a different man."

Benjamin wondered if that were true. If he *was* capable of changing.

If either of them was.

Just like his cousin, he had put walls up around his heart to keep others from getting in. Unlike his cousin, part of Benjamin now wished it didn't have to be that way.

The opening ceremony for the aviary was in just a couple hours. This would be Benjamin's last opportunity to spend time with Noelle before collecting his mother's locket and putting Cressmouth behind him. A strange emptiness filled his chest. Leaving Noelle would be harder than ever. He pushed the thought away.

Just because he could not be here for her physically did not erase a sudden need to provide for her in his absence. He doubted she would agree. Noelle did not need Benjamin's help to survive. She was smart and strong and independent. But to him, she was so much more than that. She had turned her entire town into a family. If he could give her anything at all, it would be more time to enjoy that family while she had it.

He left his cousin in the menagerie and made his way down to the temporary office the solicitor had set up in the castle in order to oversee Grandfather's last will and testament.

"Your Grace!" The solicitor leapt up from his chair. "How may I be of service?"

Benjamin took a seat across from the desk. "I would like to employ an assistant clerk for the counting house."

The solicitor's eyes widened. "You wish to replace Miss Pratchett?"

"No. I wish to employ an assistant for her," Benjamin said. "She has taken on far more responsibility than her predecessors realized, and should not be worked to death. Miss Pratchett deserves recreational time with which to do as she pleases."

"An assistant." The solicitor shuffled through the papers on his desk. "I was one of Mr. Marlowe's most trusted men of business, yet he left no notes about creating such a post. I will investigate to see if the budget—"

"*I* wish to employ," Benjamin repeated. "I will also pay whatever wages are required for the research and recruitment of potential employees. The appropriate individual must ease Miss Pratchett's load, not create additional concerns."

The solicitor nodded in comprehension. "Consider it done. I presume Your Grace wishes to have final say, once we have whittled down the options."

"Miss Pratchett shall have the only say," Benjamin said firmly. "She may employ as many assistants as she requires, at her complete and total discretion."

The solicitor noted quickly. "Understood, Your Grace. I shall see to it immediately."

Benjamin glanced at his pocket watch and rose

to his feet. He did not wish to be late for his meeting with Noelle.

In his eagerness to see her, Benjamin strode into the glasshouse a full quarter of an hour before they were due to meet.

She was there among the flowers on the other side of the vast conservatory, speaking to Miss Penelope Mitchell, her perfumer friend.

Benjamin did not care a fig about colognes, or the rows of spices for the kitchen, or the profusion of local and exotic flowers for the gardens. None of their fragrances or colors could compare to Noelle.

She was captivating. The morning light caught the sparkle in her eyes, the golden shine in her hair. Her happy, upturned face was so animated and enthusiastic he felt himself smiling from across the glasshouse without even hearing her words.

Noelle always had that effect on him. She caused him to smile when he didn't mean to, when he couldn't explain his exuberance even to himself. Being with her gave him such a profound sense of contentment it almost made him wonder if he'd ever truly been happy before he met her. Noelle *was* his glasshouse; his color, his light, his warmth. Even when winter raged out-of-doors, she made his soul feel like summertime.

He wished he could keep a ray of her sunlight with him for the rest of his days.

Although he had been careful not to make a sound, her head turned sharply as if she had sensed him watching her from afar. A wide smile spread across her face. His lips curved in an answering smile. He couldn't help it. Her pull was as powerful as the sun.

He started walking toward her.

She bid good-day to her friend and hurried forward to greet him. They met in the middle of the glasshouse, surrounded by the scent of spring and a cornucopia of wild beauty.

If only he could stay here, or steal her away when he left. But he belonged to London and she to Cressmouth. More insurmountable, she was an orphan and he was a duke. Homes could be changed, but heritage could not. Society's position on the matter was clear.

Not that Benjamin was in the market for a wife, he reminded himself. Soon enough, he'd be too busy with Parliament to have time for distractions of any kind. This was his last one.

"Did you solve your friend's problems?" he asked gruffly.

She grinned up at him, brown eyes sparkling behind gold-rimmed spectacles. "I am arranging an event to celebrate her latest success."

"Complete with an enormous bellows to spray the entire crowd?" He gave a little shudder.

"Not this time," she said with a laugh. "Customers must make do with glass vials."

"I am certain the event will be a success," he said in seriousness. "With your eye for detail, I've no doubt you are a phenomenal hostess no matter what the event."

"It's a calling," she said with a grin. "There's nothing I cannot organize."

He stared at her in silence for a moment. She *would* make a phenomenal hostess. The sort that might make an equally phenomenal duchess. If such were an option.

"Would you ever leave Cressmouth?" he asked suddenly.

"Leave?" Her eyes widened with obvious alarm. "Why would I wish to?"

"What if it wasn't a permanent change?" he pressed. "Would you not even go on holiday somewhere, once in a while?"

She shook her head. "I wouldn't like to be far away. Cressmouth has everything I need."

"It cannot compete with London," he said a bit more defensively than he intended.

London was where his mother and father had lived. The now-empty Silkridge residence contained the few happy family memories he'd ever had. It was the only place that had ever felt like home.

"London?" she stammered with the same level of terror as if he had said *snake pit*. "I wouldn't feel comfortable. Everything I've ever heard makes it sound like the opposite of Cressmouth. It's so big, so far away, so overwhelming..."

He could not fault her there. The city was indeed the opposite in many ways. Some of its characteristics negative, some of them marvelous. But his question had been answered, and the answer was no. His home would make her miserable. He would much rather keep her happy.

"How about you?" she asked. "Will you return to holiday in Cressmouth someday?"

Return to a place that contained her, only to have to leave her behind over and over again? A village that symbolized everything he could not have, now more than ever? He would not survive such a nightmare.

"I'm afraid not," he said quietly.

Noelle bit her lip as if swallowing words she wanted to say. She cast her gaze downward.

"What is it?" he demanded.

With a sigh, she lifted her eyes to his. "I know why you're leaving this time. You're a duke. You have a duty to Parliament."

He gave a curt nod.

Her next words were a whisper. "Why did you leave last time?"

"Because I wanted to stay." The hoarse admission wrested from his throat.

Her eyes widened. "You wanted to stay... with me?"

Before he spilled any more unintended confessions, he pulled her close and slanted his mouth over hers.

She yielded to him immediately, grasping his shoulders as though she feared he would pull away.

He never wished to stop. This was what he needed. The woman he missed every minute they were apart.

He had left her before due to the same sensation she instilled in his heart even now: *fear*. Fear that if he let himself be vulnerable again, he still couldn't keep her. It was not a risk he wished to take. Not a heartbreak he wished to live through.

Yet each kiss only made him want to claim more than her mouth. He wanted to taste her skin, to know her body, to meld as one.

If a single kiss could make him feel as if their souls had cleaved together, how much harder would it be to bear a lifetime without her if he risked sharing more than that?

"The eagle can fly over a hundred miles to be with its mate," mused a female voice right behind them.

Benjamin ripped his mouth from Noelle's and tried to calm his galloping heart. The avian expert had arrived.

"Virginia," Noelle said, her cheeks flushed and her voice breathless. "You're early."

"I'm half an hour late." Without demanding further explanation, Miss Underwood turned abruptly and began striding away. "This way to the partridge."

He offered her his arm, so they could hurry after her retreating friend.

Noelle gave him a shy smile that melted his heart.

"Come along," Miss Underwood called. "I've installed the partridge in the closest outbuilding in order to give you the honor of carrying him into the aviary."

He slanted a startled glance toward Noelle.

"That means you," she said quickly. "I seek no honor."

Benjamin gazed down at her. He had never met anyone more honorable.

Regardless of how she might have felt in the

beginning, she was not helping him now because she wished to be rid of him, but rather despite the fact that she did not. His spirits sank.

He had never been less enthusiastic about getting his way.

CHAPTER 10

For the first time, Cressmouth's endless winter felt less charming and more simply...cold.

Noelle tried to keep her shaking fingers from gripping too hard as she looped her arm through Silkridge's and allowed him to escort her—and the partridge—to the aviary.

The bird was cozily ensconced in a covered wicker basket hanging from the duke's other arm. Noelle felt significantly less stable. Of the two, her fluttering heart seemed more likely to fly from her chest than the bird from the basket.

It was a quarter to twelve. Within the next half hour, Silkridge would deposit the bird in the aviary, break the bottle of champagne, and be gone.

"Are you ready?" she whispered.

She wished she hadn't spoken. She already knew the answer.

"Yes," he said with a quick glance to ensure the safety of the bird inside the basket.

Noelle was not ready. She doubted she would ever be. All she could think about was the incredible kiss they had just shared. It had transported her out of the glasshouse, out of the castle, into a world of fantasy where nothing could keep them apart.

She supposed she could have delayed him artificially. He did not know her bosom friend was an expert on birds. He had not asked for her help. If anything, he had seemed perturbed that his grandfather's will had thrown them together in such a fashion. At first.

Now she was uncertain what to think.

She had no doubt that he desired her. His ardent kisses had proven that. Nor could she doubt that he liked her. He had agreed to a sleigh ride, attended a seasonal play, wore her scarf about his neck. But such moments were far from enough.

His kisses made her want *more*. To keep Cressmouth, to keep him, to have it all.

She wanted him to want to stay. To choose *her*. Having him be part of her life, part of her home, a part of her heart...

For a moment, when he had captured her in his arms, she had thought it possible. That their connection was unbreakable. That perhaps she could keep him.

But of course she could not.

Her lips twisted at the irony. A debutante would rejoice if the gentleman she fancied was a duke. For a title-less orphan like Noelle, it meant she and Silkridge were more than star-crossed. Their futures were predetermined. This forbidden spark between them might lead to a bedchamber, but never to the altar.

His was a world of power and riches and political alliances. He could not marry her if he wished to. Besides, was that even a life she would want? Noelle would never be accepted amongst those of his class. Here in Cressmouth, she was more than accepted. She was part of a family.

A distant roar of voices met their ears before the source came into sight.

He slanted her a startled look. "Is there a disturbance?"

"There's a party." Noelle did not feel like celebrating. She forced herself to smile anyway. "I had bills posted across the village, remember?"

His expression was dubious. "How many people would choose to attend the grand opening of a one-bird aviary?"

"All of them." She pointed as the queue came into view.

A long line of laughing, wind-flushed faces snaked over every inch of the snow-covered garden and down the street.

"This crowd could fill Vauxhall," he said with a chuckle.

The thought caused a pain in Noelle's chest. She had never seen Vauxhall. Never wanted to before. But she suddenly could not put the thought of being there with Silkridge out of her mind. Or the thought of him being there with someone else.

He paused just before they came into full view of the crowd and turned to face her.

"Our time is almost over," he said softly.

It always was. They were never granted more than stolen moments. She swallowed hard. "Do you remember what happened five years ago?"

"Our first kiss?" His warm gaze was intent on hers. "I've never forgotten."

Neither would she. This was torture.

"Why do you hate Christmas?" she whispered.

It was not the real question she meant, but much easier to ask than *why do you keep leaving me?*

His expression closed. "I don't wish to discuss it."

Her voice trembled. "Was it because we—"

He grabbed her hand and placed it to his chest.

"It has nothing to do with you," he said roughly. "My father and I had a reason to despise Christmas time since the year I was born. Losing him just gave me another reason. My grandfather's castle, this picturesque holiday village... You are the best thing in it."

She drew in a shuddering breath and dared to hope.

"Could you stay?" she whispered. "If there was a reason?"

As she gazed up at him, church bells began to ring the hour. Her stomach twisted. Noon. The magic was over.

He took her hand from his chest and placed it back on his elbow. "I cannot stay, no matter how many reasons I find. I belong in London, in the House of Lords. My duty is to Parliament."

She nodded dumbly. She could not hope to compete against a love of country.

She had just hoped there might be room for her, too.

CHAPTER 11

$\mathcal{B}$enjamin stood before the entrance to the aviary and faced a crowd of hundreds.

He had given any number of addresses to Parliament that ought to carry much more weight and import. But for the first time, he felt as though he stood at the crossroads of his own life.

At last, he was seconds away from washing his hands of his grandfather's final manipulation. Minutes away from once more having in his possession an heirloom he had feared lost to him forever. An hour away from being back in his carriage with which he could finally put all things Cressmouth and Christmas behind him for good.

So why hadn't he begun the proceedings?

He tried not to send another glance toward Noelle, but the temptation was impossible to resist. If he had yearned for her before, his addiction had only increased. It was as if his eyes wished to drink her up, to commit every eyelash, every wrinkle of her nose, every curve of her lips to memory.

But he was too close to having done with his grandfather's final manipulation. He could let nothing stand in its way. Especially not his own emotions.

"Welcome to the Castle Aviary Grand Opening," he called out, feeling absolutely ridiculous using such terminology to describe a single brown game bird nestled in a wicker basket.

The crowd let out a thundering cheer, as if he had announced the war with France was finally over and that he had personally defeated Napoleon Bonaparte armed with nothing more than a partridge.

They could not possibly be serious. He slid an incredulous glance toward Noelle.

"We like parties," she said with a grin. "And Mr. Marlowe. And Cressmouth. There's really no way this could go wrong."

Benjamin hoped not. Nonetheless, he lifted a corner of the blanket covering the basket to ensure he carried a partridge, not porridge, and that nothing else could go awry. The bird lay in the center, one wing covering its head as if to block out the roar from the crowd.

"My sincere apologies," Benjamin whispered. "Soon you can hide in a tree where you belong."

With a flourish, he opened the door to the aviary and whipped the blanket from the basket to allow the bird to fly inside.

The partridge did not move.

He gave the basket a little jiggle. Had the bird

expired in the hundred yards from outbuilding to aviary? God help him.

The partridge opened one baleful eye and glared sullenly at Benjamin.

His shoulders relaxed. The creature hadn't died. It just hated him.

"Behold the partridge!" Benjamin shouted and shoved the uncovered basket over the threshold and into the aviary.

Nothing happened. No chirps. Not so much as a flutter.

Benjamin ignored the bird. It was inside the aviary. That was all that mattered. The terms were complete. A thousand people could file indoors to gather around a basket if they so wished. He had fulfilled his part of the bargain.

"Champagne," murmured Noelle and gestured toward a footman.

Almost fulfilled. One last step, and his mother's locket would finally return home. Benjamin's heart was racing so fast it had become difficult to think. He accepted a ceremonial saber from one footman as another held the bottle of champagne aloft.

Benjamin did not feel like Napoleon conquering new lands. He felt... like part of the town.

He motioned everyone to back up a safe distance from the entrance and lifted the saber. "I dedicate this building to—"

"Mr. Marlowe!" the crowd screamed in unison.

Their deafening roar drowned out Benjamin's words as he met Noelle's eyes. "To the indomitable Miss Pratchett."

With a swipe of the saber, the neck's seam began to crack. A loud *pop* filled the air as the cork went flying. Foamy champagne sprayed upon the wooden doorframe and Benjamin's black boots.

His heart leaped. He'd done it!

Two footmen rushed forward to relinquish him of the saber before the stampeding crowd overtook them.

Benjamin glanced inside the aviary at the bird in the basket.

It was empty.

"Where's the partridge?" he whispered to Noelle.

"I didn't see it move," she whispered back, frowning into the interior. "It cannot have disappeared."

Benjamin gritted his teeth. He had no wish to actually enter the aviary. He did not want to be caught by the tidal wave of the crowd.

Worse, however, would be for the solicitor to cry foul and claim he had not executed his grandfather's bequest as promised. Benjamin had not come all this way to fail now.

He stalked through the entrance, scouring atop branches and behind decorative shrubs in search of the elusive bird.

The crowd poured in behind him.

Rather than follow Benjamin along the carefully curated path through the aviary's painstakingly pruned flora, they streamed to an empty corner on the opposite side of the aviary containing nothing but a plain, spindly sapling listing on its own in a bucket of dirt.

Benjamin frowned. *Had* his grandfather's will said "pear tree?"

"It's a brilliant partridge!" a voice called out.

"She looks perfectly at home," called another. "Placing her on a pear tree is a right lovely touch."

His body flooded with relief. The partridge had been spotted. The ordeal was over. He had christened the one-bird aviary with all the pomp and circumstance required of him, and was free at last to reunite with his family. The locket and its portrait could finally return home. He could be hours away by nightfall.

Benjamin darted desperate glances around the aviary in search of Noelle, but it was no use. The entire village was attempting to cram itself inside.

He would say goodbye after he retrieved the locket. Perhaps that was better anyway. Poetic. She would be the last thing he saw before he left. The only memory of this place he wished to keep.

He squeezed his way through the crowd to the exit. Once his Hessians touched the ground out-of-doors, he took off running without a backward glance. If the queueing villagers found it odd to spy a duke loping away from his own celebration, Benjamin did not care.

Only one thing mattered.

The winter chill stole the air from his lungs and the snow-covered streets slid beneath his boots. In mere moments, he arrived at the jeweler's out of breath and triumphant.

She was waiting for him behind the counter of her jewelry room.

His heart was pounding. "The aviary is open."

Miss Parker's eyes crinkled. "I heard."

Even from several blocks away, the crowd's excitement was audible.

He stepped forward. "May I—"

"Here." She retrieved a thin silk pouch from a hidden nook.

He held out his hands, surprised they were not trembling. He had prevailed. He had *won*.

Miss Parker upended the pouch and dropped its contents into Benjamin's outstretched palm.

He had promised himself he would immediately clasp the locket about his neck for safekeeping, but he needed to gaze upon his mother's face once more. The hollowness he'd carried inside all these years would fill with love once more. With family. He unlocked the clasp and opened the locket.

There. Faded with time, but finally back in his hands. His pulse slowed. He should be full of warmth, of victory. The emptiness should have receded. He had everything he always wanted.

And yet the hollowness remained.

"Is something amiss?" asked the jeweler with concern.

He snapped the locket closed. "Nothing. Thank you for giving me my family back. I will take good care of them."

Before she could ask any more questions, Benjamin strode out of her workroom and back out onto the front stoop. The blustery wind blew over the village and through his chest.

He lifted the chain to his throat and clasped it about his neck.

No. This would not do.

He unwound the scarf, untied his cravat, and slid the gold oval underneath his shirt until it nestled against his heart. He frowned.

The locket's return should warm him more than any scarf, than any cravat, and any amount of wool or cozy fire. Instead, he felt cold. Every gust of wind seemed icier than the one before, penetrating his great coat and his waistcoat and his linen shirt until it sliced all the way through his soul.

He curled his hands into fists and glared up at the relentless blue sky. Why hadn't the return of the locket given him all the things he had hoped it would bring? He had his family back. He had his mother right next to his heart.

But the portrait's return failed to vanquish the loneliness and emptiness and resentfulness. The locket bore a permanent place about his neck, but failed to fill the hole in his chest. The heirloom was a memento he would always cherish, but still just a *thing*.

His breath shuddered. Now that he had the locket back, he realized the awful truth. A portrait was just paint, no matter how much he might like to believe otherwise. It didn't erase the pain. His mother's likeness could not replicate the real person. The happy family in the miniature would never exist again. What it represented was long gone, just like both his parents.

His chest clenched. What was better, to cleave to a faded likeness or to keep loved ones close while one still had them? The answer was clear.

He wrapped the scarf Noelle had made him back around his neck and cut through the wind toward the castle. She was the one person he could rely on. He was not yet ready for goodbye.

When he drew close, the aviary was still bursting at the seams. Villagers spilled across its threshold and milled about the garden. Benjamin doubted Noelle was among the revelers. She was one of the few who hadn't been looking forward to the aviary's opening.

He circled around the bustling crowd and entered the vacant castle. Nothing but silence greeted him. Benjamin's footfalls echoed as he raced up six flights of steps to Noelle's chamber.

When she opened the door, he pulled her into his arms and kissed her. He couldn't have stopped himself if he wanted to. The heat of her mouth was the only warmth he required. Her embrace, more than enough protection from the cold. Nothing else mattered but holding her tight.

At last, he forced himself to lift his head. "May I come in?"

"Please do." With a blush, she shut the door behind him and gestured toward a receiving area before the fire.

His nerves were far too raw for sitting down, but he followed her anyway. He was not ready to let her out of his sight.

Her eyes were full of questions. He no longer believed he had any answers.

"Silkridge…" she began.

"Benjamin," he said firmly. "I've no wish to stand on formalities with you of all people."

"What do you want?" she said quietly.

You.

Happiness.

A new life. A different world. One where they could be together. Anything but this.

He tossed his hat onto the closest chair and shoved a hand through his hair.

Noelle gazed up at him uncertainly from behind her spectacles. "I thought you went to fetch the locket."

"I did."

The words sounded as cold and hollow as the yawning cavern in his chest. Nothing about today had gone as planned. Now that he was here, what could he expect but more heartache?

Her fingertips brushed against the back of his hand. "What happened?"

"It's what didn't happen," he said at last. "I thought…"

Her gaze softened. "Start at the beginning."

"I can't remember the beginning," he said bitterly. But he forced the words out anyway. "My mother died shortly after giving birth to me. That was my first Christmastide. The only one where I had a family. The last time my father celebrated anything at all."

Her eyes widened in understanding. "You never had a Christmas."

"Not one I'd wish to repeat. I lost my father during the same time of year, and just as suddenly." He let out a shaky breath. "Everyone I have ever loved has been taken from me before I could say goodbye."

"Is that why…" she began hesitantly. "…the locket means so much?"

"It's more than a locket."

He lay his great coat and scarf over the back of an armchair and tossed his cravat atop the seat.

His neck felt bare. Exposed. But he was about to expose even more. He lifted the locket from beneath the linen of his shirt and allowed it to fall back against his chest.

"It's beautiful." She lifted her hands as if to touch the gold frame then let them fall without doing so. Her eyes met his.

"Open it," he said. "You can meet my mother."

Gently, she slid her hand between the locket and his chest and undid the clasp.

He held his breath.

From this angle, he could not see the portrait inside, but he had committed it to memory. At this moment, he was not looking at the locket. He was looking at Noelle.

"You look like your mother," she murmured. "You have her eyes."

His throat grew tight. They wouldn't recognize him now. "I suppose I've grown a bit since that portrait was painted."

A soft smile curved her lips. "You'll have to hang this next to your most recent likeness in your hall of portraits."

He didn't answer.

Her brow furrowed. "You haven't a hall of portraits? I thought all titled families…"

"There aren't any of me," he said. Just the thought gave him chills. "After my mother died, my father never posed for another portrait. Neither did I."

Her eyes widened, and she returned her reverent gaze to the locket. "This miniature truly is beautiful. I hope it has brought you the peace that you sought."

"It didn't." Somehow, he kept his voice from cracking.

She glanced up sharply. "It wasn't as you remembered it?"

"It was exactly as I remembered," he said. "And nothing more. I thought... I was certain..."

She touched the locket's delicate frame. "How did you lose it?"

"What I lost was my family. The locket was *stolen* from me. My grandfather felt he had more claim to his daughter than a child did of his own mother."

She drew in her breath. "That's why you hated him."

"I didn't hate him. He hated me." Benjamin took a deep breath. "Mother died of complications caused by my birth. She barely lasted a month. That was my fault."

"It was *not* your fault," Noelle said sharply, her eyes fierce.

"Tell that to Grandfather," he said with a curl of his lip. "I always thought if I could get the locket back, I could get my family back. Part of them, anyway. This was the one piece I had. The only tangible thing I could hold onto."

"Until he took it," she murmured quietly. "That must have hurt deeply."

It had been devastating. This was the first time Benjamin had ever spoken about how it had felt. His pulse felt wild and uneven.

"I should have expected it," he admitted. "Grandfather despised me from the moment of my birth. He blamed my father, too. I was a child. I didn't understand. All I knew was that my mother was gone, but I still had a grandfather. My letters went unanswered, he was suddenly too busy to be disturbed any time Father brought me for a visit. As I got older, I realized he had no interest in getting to know me. He wished I hadn't been born."

Noelle gasped. "Surely he would never wish—"

"He said so to my face," Benjamin said flatly. "That was my mistake, too. When he invited me five years ago, I should have suspected a trap. It turned out, he'd learned of the locket. I was so eager to finally make peace, of course I handed it over when he asked for a closer look. That was the last time I saw it. Grandfather threw me out of the castle—"

"Threw out his own grandson?" she said in shock. "A duke?"

"I wasn't a duke yet, and he didn't give two figs about his grandson. He had what he wanted, and it wasn't me."

"That was… the day after our kiss?" she asked.

Benjamin nodded. "I never came back."

"You weren't allowed back." Her eyes flashed. "Your grandfather wouldn't let you."

He lifted a shoulder. "Either way, I've come to regret it."

She tilted her head. "You think things would

have worked out differently if you had tried to visit your grandfather again?"

"Not him." Benjamin stepped closer. "I regret all those years without seeing you. At the very least, we deserved a chance to say goodbye."

"You didn't get to say goodbye to your grandfather, either," she said quietly.

"I've never got to say goodbye to anyone I care about." His chest tightened at the barrage of memories. "I can't let it happen again."

She lowered her gaze. "That's why you're here."

"Not the only reason." He couldn't stay away. That was the problem.

He was not used to making confessions of any kind. Had insulated himself on purpose so that he would not ever be in a position where he was expected to slice open his heart and bare what he kept inside.

With her, he felt even more vulnerable. But she was different. Noelle did not judge him or shower him with platitudes. She simply listened and understood.

He had never known how powerful such a simple act could be.

His heart thumped wildly against the back of her hand where she held the locket. The miniature inside was his most prized possession. Its protective gold housing symbolized not just family, but love.

The blank spots on the other side of his mother's face had been meant for a new portrait. His own, perhaps. It was now destined to remain empty. He had vowed to never again risk his heart on something so fleeting as love or family, but if he ever were to do so…

He reached behind his neck and unclasped the chain.

The locket pooled into Noelle's open palm and she glanced up at him, startled. "I didn't mean for you to—"

Her words cut off as Benjamin reached behind her neck and reaffixed the clasp.

Now the locket lay not against his heart, but hers.

"Don't give up on having a family," she whispered.

"I'm not," he answered and pulled her into his arms.

This kiss was different from all the others. Neither a claiming nor a submission, but a flaying open, a laying bare. This kiss was who he was. His hopes, his fears, his grief, his desire. He hoped he could make her understand.

Benjamin had not given up on his family. His grandfather had closed himself off. His parents had been stolen away to heaven. That was it. There was no one left to give up on. No reason for hope at all.

Noelle's kisses had made him yearn for a happy ending. That a wish could come true, that vulnerability could bring joy instead of grief. That love did not merely have to be a symbol, but rather something real and true and lasting.

But he knew better.

When he broke the kiss, it was as if a piece of his heart broke with it. He had to get out of Cressmouth. Away from the false hope of endless Christmas. Everything about it reminded him of anger and loss. Everything except her.

He did not agree with Society's view that an orphan like Noelle was beneath him and unworthy. But his feelings didn't matter. As a duke, he was forced to operate within that society. To make deals and alliances. To uphold conventions and expectations.

He could promise her nothing but heartbreak.

"I can't stay," he whispered hoarsely.

She nodded. "I know. I've always known."

"I never wanted to leave you," he said hoarsely, lest she doubt the demons that drove him. "I had to leave this town. I still do. It reminds me..."

She reached up to caress his cheek.

He leaned into her warmth. "I have no good Christmas memories."

"Until now." She wrapped her hands around his neck. "Let's make some new ones."

His heart thumped and he crushed his mouth to hers.

Perhaps she was right. The past was the past. It was time to make new memories. Time to risk lowering his guard, if only for a moment.

Tonight was all they could ever have.

His blood raced. What would it be like to let go of all the old fear, all the shame and anger, and give himself over to the moment completely? Could exposing his heart bring more joy than he'd ever believed possible?

Or would making himself vulnerable to intimacy cut even deeper?

CHAPTER 12

*N*oelle swayed as her runaway pulse pounded through her veins. She wrapped her arms about Benjamin and held on tight, the locket about her neck now sheltered between two hearts instead of one. Perhaps then they could be whole.

She did not blame him for the estranged relationship with his grandfather. Nor could she blame him for the resulting distaste for all things Cressmouth and Christmas.

Her heart dipped in sympathy. They had both lost their parents. It was not an easy thing to get over.

Noelle had never had a family portrait before, or any relic of her parents whatsoever. Had she possessed such a priceless heirloom, she would have cherished it above all others. No wonder Benjamin had done the same.

By entrusting his most treasured possession to her keeping, it was as though he was sharing his family with her. As if she too were deserving of such love. As if Noelle held equal weight in his heart.

How could she help but love him?

Her pulse skipped in warning. It was no longer a suspicion in the back of her mind. She was hopelessly, madly, deeply in love with a man who would leave her behind. Abandon her, just as her own parents had done.

No. Not as her parents had done. They had left no sign, no word, no token of affection. Benjamin was *here*. His lips pressed to hers, his tongue hot and demanding. From any other man, a locket would be nothing more than a piece of jewelry. In Benjamin's case, he had given her his heart.

At least, as much as he was willing to part with.

Could she not do the same? She yearned to reveal herself to him, body and soul. The thought of such a risk terrified her now more than ever, but this was their last opportunity.

"I thought you didn't want me," she whispered against his mouth.

He raised his head sharply, his gaze intense. "I pushed you away not because I don't want you, but because I cannot keep you. Yet I long for you like a sapling longs for rain. Although I know I cannot stay, I long to touch you, to taste you, to feel you against my skin."

Noelle's lungs caught. She had known he would not offer empty promises. Those words were simultaneously the most romantic and the most devastating thing he could have said to her.

The golden locket about her neck was the reason he had returned to Cressmouth. The locket was the reason he was here in her arms right now. It was his heart, divided into halves. One side contained the past. The other side was for the future.

They had both seen that the future was empty. But today did not have to be.

She wanted Benjamin more than anything under the sun. Their differences might be irreconcilable, but she wouldn't let that stop her from enjoying him for as long as she could.

"I never stopped thinking of you," she confessed between kisses. "Night after night, replaying your touch in my mind. Your kiss. Wondering what else we might have shared if we'd had time."

His dark gaze was tortured. "It isn't just time that divides us. If it weren't for everything that lies outside these walls, I would make love to you all night."

A delicious shiver slid down her spine. She sank her fingers into his hair to pull him close. "Then why don't you?"

His mouth claimed hers, his hands cupping her bottom to pull her tight against him. "Because you deserve so much more than I can give."

He was trying to scare her away. It wouldn't work. Noelle already knew the end of the story and was choosing him anyway. If her heart was destined to break, she would take every bit of pleasure while she still could.

"Give what you can," she whispered. "Take what you please."

His breath was ragged. "Noelle—"

"One night," she said as she tasted his lips. "Unless you aren't interested."

"*All* I want is you," he growled. "But if I cannot offer marriage, I certainly cannot rob you of your virginity."

"You cannot steal what is freely given," she reminded him.

"It's not honorable," he said, want and indecision warring in his eyes. "A gentleman wouldn't—"

"—say 'no' to a lady. Especially not if it's what he wants, too." She cupped his cheek. "If there won't be a second chance, shouldn't we take the one we have?"

He kissed the inside of her palm, her wrist, her lips. "Being with you is the one thing that makes me happy."

She wrapped her arms about his neck. "Don't we deserve one night of happiness together?"

"One night. Just for us." He lifted her in his strong arms.

She held on tight. "A night to remember."

In a few swift strides, they reached the bedchamber and tumbled atop the bed.

She pushed all thought of losing him out of her head and immersed herself in the current moment. The soft down of her bed. The hard muscle in his body. The bright crackle of the fire. The matching flame deep inside her.

Her heart soared higher with each kiss. She had dreamed of this, dreamed of him. The weight of his body pressed against her. She thrilled at the sensation, at the knowledge that soon she would know him more intimately than she had ever dreamed.

When he slid to one side, separating from her, she tried to break the kiss to complain about the loss. Before she could do so, his hand lifted her breast from its bodice and words failed her completely. She felt beautiful. Cherished.

Her fingers dug into the mattress with pleasure as he toyed with her bosom. Each touch of her nipple sent waves of desire through her body. This was what she had longed for. True connection.

When he moved his mouth down to her exposed breasts, she flung her arms up over her head and arched into him. She gave her body to him and in return he aroused her more than she had believed possible. It was all she could do not to claw the clothes from their bodies.

As he teased her bosom with his mouth, he tugged the hems of her skirts from her ankles to her hips. She gasped at the sensation of cool air against her exposed skin, of his hot mouth over her nipple. When his hand cupped between her legs and dipped in teasing circles, her body responded at once. She gripped his shoulders, digging her fingernails into the material to ensure he did not cease his ministrations.

A tightness was uncurling deep inside her. A fullness, a wanting. Every lick of his tongue, every flick and dip of his finger brought her closer and closer to the edge. Every time he gave, she wanted more. It was heaven and torture twisted into one. Her body pulsed with need. Something was happening. Something like...

All at once, she could withstand the delicious pressure no longer and shattered against his fingers.

"More," she gasped when she finally caught her breath. "Not your hand. I want *you*."

He covered her mouth with his as he unbuttoned the fall of his breeches. At once, the weight of his shaft fell against her, hot and heavy, nestled perfectly against the juncture of her thighs. He reached between them, as if making certain she was ready for him.

She was more than ready. She was impatient. She wanted to give him the same pleasure he had given her. She wanted to find an even greater peak together.

As he eased into her, inch by inch, she wrapped her legs about him and brought him closer, deeper. Not just into her body, but into her heart. Into her soul.

The sharp stab of pain as he entered her was quickly replaced by renewed desire. Her pulse raced as she lost herself in his kiss.

Joining with him was more than she dreamed. But when he rocked his hips and started to move... She held on tight, allowing the sensations to run through her, opening herself to him completely, taking everything he had been trying so hard not to give. In return, she would share everything she had.

If only for one night.

CHAPTER 13

*N*oelle awoke alone. When she stretched her arm out toward Benjamin, there was nothing beside her but cold linen and an empty bed. Her breath shuddered.

The wind outside whistled through cracks between the windowpanes, indicating the weather outside was as turbulent as her heart. She pushed her leaden feet off the edge of the bed and forced herself to the window. The glass was almost covered in frost. Snow was falling too deep and fast for any tracks to be visible in the streets below. There was no sign of Benjamin.

Perhaps he was halfway to London. Perhaps he was just down the corridor in his chamber, arranging for his trunk to be loaded into his carriage. Preparing to abandon her a second time. Her fingers shook with panic.

She forced her gaze from the window and sucked in a deep breath. Benjamin was incapable of abandoning her. Only someone who had made a commitment to stay could abandon another person. They had both been careful to make no such statements. There had been no promises. Benjamin was behaving exactly as he had warned from the start. If she didn't want her heart broken, it had been up to her to prevent it from becoming involved.

Besides, his departure today had nothing to do with last night, she reminded herself. A duke like Benjamin had duties, responsibilities, all sorts of things that were more important than her. Noelle's stomach twisted. Who knew? Maybe her parents had also had better things to do. More important priorities than keeping an unwanted daughter. She should be used to being alone by now. Of course Benjamin must return to his real life.

A life that didn't include her.

She touched her trembling fingers to her chest. The golden locket did not feel cold, but warm. Heated from her flesh, her dreams, this nightmare. It seemed to pulse against her skin as if it had a heartbeat of its own.

By giving her the locket, Benjamin had given up the thing that he loved most. Surely she was strong enough to do the same. No matter how it hurt. After all, that was the deal she had made. One night. Nothing more.

With listless movements, she cleaned her face at the basin and put on a day gown. She did not feel like freshening up or going anywhere at all. But what she wanted even less was a protracted goodbye with the man she loved.

Having to stand before him as he made his rejection official would be more than she could bear. Even if she'd known to expect it all along.

She wrapped herself in her warmest pelisse and fled from her bedchamber, from the castle, from anywhere she might spy Benjamin leaving her for good. That was the only defense she had left.

If they did not say goodbye, if the words were never spoken, perhaps it would be as though their parting had never happened. As if their story was not yet over. As if she could hold onto a small part of last night, a small part of *him* forever.

Even if it was all a lie.

CHAPTER 14

*B*enjamin was desperate.

He had searched everywhere in the castle for Noelle and couldn't find her anywhere. After he had slipped out to order her favorite breakfast, she was no longer in the bedchamber where he'd left her. Nor was she up in the counting house working on journals. She wasn't in the breakfast room, the glasshouse, the aviary...

She had vanished without a trace.

"Your Grace?" a footman murmured. "Your carriage is ready."

Of course his coach was ready. Benjamin had summoned it two hours ago, when he had believed Noelle was awaiting him in her chambers. But she was not there, she was not anywhere, and he was standing at the castle exit with his heart bleeding out of his chest. He *had* to say goodbye.

Yet he could not dally any longer. He should not even have stayed last night. At this point, he would have to race south, stopping for fresh horses as often as possible, to have a prayer of reaching London in time to be in his seat when the current session of Parliament began.

"Your Grace?" the footman tried again, his voice hesitant. "Should we have your driver return the coach to—"

"No. I'm going now." Benjamin whirled away from the empty receiving hall and strode outside into blinding sunlight.

Some might consider Cressmouth at its most picturesque with a fine layer of snow dusting every surface and even more snowflakes drifting lazily from the skies. Benjamin was not fooled by its beauty. This morning's high winds had been warning enough. He needed to get off this mountain and back to a main road as quickly as possible. Even if it meant leaving without seeing Noelle.

He climbed up into his coach and took his place against the plush squab. His hands should not be shaking. He had known this moment would come. Had been looking forward to leaving Cressmouth behind.

Now it felt as though he was leaving the most important part of himself behind with it.

He swung his gaze from the empty heavens to the castle. There lay another hard truth. Grandfather might have kept the locket from him all these years, but the old man had never possessed the power to deprive Benjamin of loved ones.

That was something he had been achieving on his own.

He signaled his driver and the horses started off down the snow-packed lanes. Soon Benjamin would be home. His chest should not feel this empty. He had known attachments could not last. His mother's gold locket had proven love was only a symbol, not something he was destined to keep. Just like Noelle. He was glad he had given her the locket. She was just as dear to him as the people inside. And destined to remain far out of reach.

The wind picked up force. He ignored it. No matter how low the temperature dropped, it was far colder in his heart. A wise man would lower his shields for no one, but Benjamin feared it was too late for that. The drawbridge had already been breached. Noelle was inside.

Any more time with her, and the damage would be irreversible. His soul would be inextricably linked to hers. Retreating while he still could was the only way to protect his heart.

If there were any pieces left unbroken.

The castle slipped from view. He tried not to feel the loss. There was no room in his life for sentimentality. He was expected to speak on a new law within a week. To meet with a half dozen committees dedicated to improving the lives of people all over England. That was his priority. His *duty*. How could a man in his position possibly choose one person over many, no matter how much he loved her?

He almost slid out of his seat in shock. *He loved her.*

Bloody hell. It was too late for defensive measures. He had not fortified his shields in time. Precisely as he had feared, his soul was bound to hers —and he still had to leave.

He tightened his fists in his lap. This desperation clawing through his chest proved the point. If he married Noelle, he would want to spend every moment of his time with her, wherever she might be. That wasn't a choice. Such a union would either mean shirking his duties to Parliament or his commitment to his wife.

Neither outcome was acceptable. He could not force Noelle to London only to leave her in an empty home while he spent all his time in the Palace of Westminster, embroiled in endless committees. Besides, she had no wish to leave Cressmouth. He had asked her. She had been clear.

The carriage clopped by a merry red sign partially dusted with snow:

Thank you for visiting Christmas!

His gut twisted in revulsion. Was it any wonder he hated the holiday festive season? All it had ever brought him was loss.

This time, he had caused the loss himself.

Driving away and leaving Noelle behind wasn't allowing him to return to his old life. It was destroying an alternate one. A better life he couldn't have.

His heart clenched with longing as he thought of how sweet she had looked in the morning light, sleeping softly by his side. She was an angel.

A sudden drop of ice pierced him inside at the realization of what he had done.

He had hurt her so badly the first time he had left, never to return. Now he was doing it all over again. No wonder she was avoiding him, as though he didn't exist. As if the passion they had shared was meaningless. Soon, it would be.

All that would be left was the imprint each had left behind.

CHAPTER 15

The further Benjamin got from Cressmouth, the emptier he felt inside. The long empty path ahead seemed both physical and metaphorical. How he hated that he hadn't been able to find Noelle before he left! One more separation without a goodbye in a long, sad history of regret.

The snow swirling all around him evoked the sleigh ride they had shared. The frosted tips of the evergreens lining the road reminded him of how warm it had been in that glasshouse when he'd finally given into temptation and kissed her. He was a long way from home and the distance was getting further with every mile.

At that thought, his chest tightened. When he had clasped the locket about Noelle's neck, he wasn't giving her his heart. *She* was his heart. The locket was now just an object, but she was everything. And he had been forced to leave her behind.

The horses slowed as they pulled the carriage over a narrow bridge. It felt as though he were crossing not just a stream, but from one life to another. From laughter to loneliness. From Noelle... to nothing.

His stomach twisted. Returning to London should not feel like a part of him was dying. He was being responsible. He was performing his duty.

Yet all he could think about was Noelle. Watching her giggle and tear up at a play she had seen a dozen times. The mirth on her face when they realized Mr. Fawkes had delivered a pear tree instead of a partridge. The way she had teased him about goats and birds and perfume. How brilliant she was. The counting house, how helpful she was to her friends, how quickly she had arranged the opening ceremony for the aviary. His breath grew shallow.

Every moment of the northern holiday he had never wished to take, Noelle had stood by his side. She had done much more than make it bearable. Whether they were laughing together, working together, or making love together, she filled his heart with joy. He was his happiest when he was with her. *She* was the missing piece he had been looking for all along.

And now she was gone. His heart banged against his chest in protest.

The driver picked up speed. This far from Cressmouth, the snow had disappeared. The ground was no longer frozen. The steeds carried them further, faster. No matter what Benjamin's heart might want. He rubbed his face.

The only person he could blame for leaving

Noelle behind was himself. This morning, he had chosen to summon his horses, climb in his carriage, return to London. But he'd put up his walls long before that. Years ago when they'd shared their first kiss, he had already become cold and inaccessible.

This time was worse. He had shut her out of his heart when all he wanted was to let her inside. She made him a better person. Her willingness and ability to force him out from where he was most comfortable had been good for him. Good for them. She enriched his life.

And she didn't even *know*.

He slumped back against the squab. He had been a fool to leave without telling her. Without explaining how much she meant. Even if he returned for occasional visits… it would be far less than she deserved. Far less than he wanted.

He touched the scarf about his neck. The one Noelle had knitted for him, even before he had given her a reason to forgive him, much less trust him. All he'd given her in return were more reasons to lose faith in him all over again. All in the name of England.

The road widened as the carriage exited the forest and clattered out between wide swaths of farmland. At this pace, they would make it to the first posting-house in no time. Be in London earlier than expected. One more face amongst the many. An automaton serving the House of Lords and nothing more.

Was this who he wished to be? Cold, dutiful, emotionless? He was not that man anymore, if he ever truly had been. He would have to do better. Noelle deserved so much more than he'd been able to give.

Sharp, familiar fear pricked the edges of his mind. The terrible conviction that if he opened himself up, if he let himself love, if he admitted the truth out loud, he would lose her anyway. He drew in a shallow breath.

Weren't some things worth everything? Wasn't Noelle worth the risk?

For so long, Benjamin had believed he would be worth nothing as a gentleman if he did not give his all to the House of Lords. He now suspected the lowlier man would be the featherwit who let the chance of the love of a lifetime slip away yet again.

What use was being the hero of Parliament, if he could not be a hero to the woman he loved most?

With a sudden movement, he signaled the driver to stop the coach at once.

The horses halted obediently. It was Benjamin's heartbeat that ran amok.

Carefully, the horses turned the carriage about in the slippery lane and headed back in the direction they had come. He urged the driver to make haste.

Winning Noelle back wouldn't be easy. Perhaps he was already too late. He had left her twice. She might be unwilling to try a third time. But it didn't matter. He had to try. She was worth any risk at any price. *Love* was worth it.

The horses raced back up the narrow path

curving around the mountain. There would be no return toward London today. By the time the beasts would arrive at the castle, they would be too exhausted to continue on.

Benjamin didn't *want* to continue on. Not alone. He wanted Noelle. He needed her to know how much he loved her. How much he regretted every moment without her. How he hoped never to part again. He had to get to her. Snow sprayed from the wheels of the carriage as he took curve after curve.

Mr. Fawkes was right. It *was* better to have loved and lost than never to have loved at all... But it was even better to get his imbecilic arse back to Cressmouth posthaste and do his damnedest not to lose Noelle.

He knew how much she loved her mountain village, how much a part of her it was. She had no reason to trust him. She might not wish to share her life with him even if she believed his heart was true.

Perhaps the issues weren't insurmountable. He would beg her hand and find a way. Although he couldn't promise himself solely to Cressmouth, he could promise himself to her. Even if he turned out not to be enough, Noelle was worth fighting for.

He had to try.

CHAPTER 16

*N*oelle sat at Penelope's dining nook with one elbow propped upon the table and her chin in her hand. Although her dear friend did her best to distract her with impassioned scientific explanations about the chemical compounds in her newest perfume, nothing could keep Noelle's mind from Benjamin. No quantity of piping hot tea could chase away the endless chill inside her heart.

The moment she let her guard down, her worst fear came true. She had been seated right here at Penelope's breakfast table when the coach with his ducal crest had rolled by.

He had left her, exactly as her parents had done. Just like she had expected. She had known not to believe it could be different this time. It was not his fault.

She could not accuse him of raising false hopes. Making love had been her idea. More than an idea, it had been an intimacy she had yearned to share with him for so long. If she was feeling melancholy because she hadn't been strong enough to say goodbye, it was no one's fault but hers.

Her lungs froze in sudden horror.

Was lack of goodbye not the precise situation that had hurt Benjamin the most, time and again? The very reason the locket about her neck was so precious to him was because everyone he ever cared about had been ripped from him before he had a chance to say goodbye.

His family had not meant to leave him so abruptly.

Noelle had done it by design.

She lowered her face into her hands.

"Are you all right?" Penelope asked softly.

Noelle pushed to her feet. "I have to go."

She could not impose on Penelope any longer.

In minutes, Noelle was bundled against the cold and trudging back toward the castle, back toward the empty counting house and her lonely bedchamber, back toward the rest of her life. One without Benjamin.

Perhaps loneliness was her destiny. It was no one's fault Benjamin had been born heir to a dukedom. No one's fault his primary seat was miles away. No one's fault his duty was to the House of Lords. If she wished to be angry, it might as well be with the stars above.

From the moment he'd come back, she'd known she could expect nothing from him.

And yet he'd managed to surprise her anyway.

The comfortable chair and better lighting in the counting house. His repeated kindnesses with

Mr. Fawkes, no matter how many misunderstandings. The way Benjamin had made Tiny Tim's health his personal responsibility. How he'd let her shove him into a sleigh and sit through a festive play despite all the pain Christmas had brought him.

He'd done it all for Noelle. Because he wanted to be with her, while it was possible.

She strode through the castle entrance and headed toward the counting house stairs. Perhaps journals and accounts would keep her mind from Benjamin better than tea with a well-meaning friend. At least she could make herself useful.

"Miss Pratchett," a male voice called just as she reached the winding staircase.

She turned around to find Mr. Marlowe's solicitor smiling at her. "May I help you?"

"I should say so." He nodded with satisfaction. "We've no less than eight candidates for your review. I've taken the liberty of inquiring into their references for you."

She stared at him blankly. "Candidates for what?"

"The apprenticeship, of course. One moment, miss." The solicitor fetched a stack of papers from his office. "Here we are. His Grace arranged for you to have an assistant. As I've stated—"

"What if I don't want an assistant?" she stammered.

"Then don't pick one," the solicitor replied. "His Grace was quite clear on the matter. You alone have the authority to select as few or as many apprentices as you deem fit for the counting house."

"*I* have the authority," she repeated. "*Me.*"

The solicitor nodded. "Every decision left to your sole and complete discretion, miss. If you'd like me to search for different candidates—"

"I'll take the list," she said quickly and stepped forward to accept the documents.

Her pulse pounded. Benjamin had recognized how much work it had taken to clear up the old records and put them to rights. He had warned her not to spend so much time in the counting house that there was no room left in her days for life.

This was his way of letting her have everything she wanted. A position of acknowledged importance as well as the freedom to take time for herself. She held the papers to her chest. With the right staff in place, the counting house would function whether Noelle was absent for an afternoon or an extended holiday.

The corner of her mouth curved. Whether he liked Christmas or not, Benjamin had managed to provide both for Noelle and for the villagers. He had ensured less work for her and created new positions for others. He had left Cressmouth a better place.

"How is Tiny Tim?" she asked suddenly.

The solicitor didn't blink at the sudden change in topic. "As neat as ninepence, miss. Jumping all over everything again. A new lease on life, I'd say."

Noelle took a deep breath. The pygmy goat

wasn't the only one who felt like leaping for joy. It was time for her to change as well.

As long as she only viewed herself as a function of Cressmouth, there was no room in her overextended life for anyone else. Not even Benjamin. She was equally responsible for pushing him away. For not making room. For being a fool.

Cressmouth would be right here all year round... but Noelle didn't have to be.

If she was willing to try.

Her hands shook as she pointed out a pair of names to the solicitor. "These two look promising. How soon can they start?"

"They're here now, miss." He gestured toward his makeshift office. "Both have years of experience with accounting. Shall I send them up to familiarize themselves with ours?"

"Send Mr. Fawkes up, too. He'll enjoy sharing the castle's history as he acquaints them with the accounts."

"As you please, miss. Should I tell them you'll be up shortly?"

"No," she said slowly, her resolve strengthening. "I don't think I will be."

When Benjamin had asked if she would be willing to visit London, she had dismissed the idea out of hand. But he hadn't been trying to take something away from her. He was trying to offer her something *more*.

She had been wrong to judge her self-worth on her loyalty to her village. Leaving its borders for a time wouldn't mean she loved it any less. He had come here, to a place filled with ghosts and bad memories. Surely she could survive a trip south to an unfamiliar city.

Her heart pounded. She didn't want to let go of Benjamin. She wanted to hold on tight. Only together would they be whole.

She shoved the documents into the solicitor's hands and spun back toward the castle exit.

He stepped aside and clasped the papers to his chest in bafflement. "Where are you going, miss?"

To Benjamin. There was no time to waste.

"I need to see a lady about a horse," she called over her shoulder and ran out the door.

Outside, the weather was just as cold as before, but no longer felt so bleak. This time it seemed the winds of change, a breeze of possibility hurrying her along her way.

Her pulse raced with urgency.

Noelle had no carriage of her own and Cressmouth was too small a village to have a plethora of hackneys one could hire in order to chase after a lost love. She would have to make do on horseback.

She slipped on a patch of ice and caught herself on a wooden pillar as she skidded off the street and onto the famous Harper stud farm.

Olive was in the barn tightening a leather tack when Noelle arrived.

"Horse," Noelle panted. "Please."

Olive looked at her doubtfully. "I've just saddled up Earl. He won't be a sedate ride. He's been restless all day and—"

"Perfect," Noelle said quickly, grateful Olive

was the sort of friend who didn't ask questions. "I'll have him back by nightfall."

Probably.

"Earl is a full-grown pony. He hasn't an assigned bedtime," Olive said with a smile as she pushed a mounting block beside him. "Good luck."

Noelle glanced at her friend sharply, then launched herself into the sidesaddle. Perhaps the real reason Olive hadn't asked any questions was because she had already surmised the answers.

"Thank you," she said and meant it. "For everything."

Olive moved the mounting block out of the way and gestured toward the open road. "Go and get him."

Noelle turned into the wind and gave Earl his head.

Benjamin might have had a two-hour head start, but he was also pulling a heavy coach. A single rider on a fast pony ought to be able to make up the same distance in half the time.

Noelle blinked falling snowflakes from her eyelashes and held on tight. She had to do more than merely catch up with Benjamin. She had to let him know how much he meant. How much she would love to stay together. How she was even willing to give him a proper goodbye, if that was what he preferred.

Just as she began to suspect her limbs had frozen to the back of the pony, she caught sight of a distant carriage ahead, a coal-black smudge in a world filled with white.

It wasn't the coach she was searching for, however. This carriage wasn't leaving Cressmouth. It was heading right toward her at breakneck speed.

She coaxed Earl to the side of the road to allow the carriage to pass.

When the driver drew close, he halted the horses and a well-dressed gentleman leapt out of the coach right before her eyes.

Benjamin. Her heart soared. He had come back for her!

"I love you," he said before she could open her mouth. "I didn't tell you when I could, so I'm telling you now. I love you, Noelle Pratchett. I'll never tire of saying so."

All the cold and numbness left her legs as she gazed down at him speechlessly.

"Tell me one thing." He stared up at her, his eyes beseeching. "Why did you hide from me?"

"Goodbye was too final," she said, her voice cracking. "I loved you and you left me anyway. I didn't want it to be over. I couldn't… I can't… You weren't…"

"I'm right here." He held out his arms and she slid down into them. "I came back. I don't want to go anywhere without you."

"Neither do I," she whispered.

He wrapped his scarf around them both, holding on tight. "You love me?"

"Of course I do, you dreadful beast." She snuggled her cheek into his warm chest.

He lifted her chin and forced her to meet his eyes.

"Come with me," he said urgently. "Let me show you a different kind of season. We can fill up the coach with anything you want to bring, and I'll arrange everything else."

"Leave Cressmouth?" Her voice might wobble, but her heart was sure. She would go anywhere to be with him. All he had to do was ask.

"As my wife," he said quickly. "Come as my duchess. Let me be your husband."

"I will never fit in with the beau monde," she stammered. "I'm an orphan..."

"So am I," he said with a crooked smile. "And who cares what they think? I don't want to fit in with the *ton*. I want to fit together with you. To marry *you*. When we start our family, we'll raise our children to know they are loved."

"And Christmas?" she asked, her heart pounding with joy.

"A lovely village," he answered without hesitation. "We can spend half the year here, and half the year in London. What do you think?" His eyes were beseeching. "Mightn't it be the best of both worlds?"

"No." She wound her arms about his neck to give him a kiss. "It'll be the best of both seasons."

He grinned. "That means yes?"

"It means I'll go anywhere, as long as I'm with you." She kissed the tip of his nose. "After all, why have one home when we could have two?"

CHAPTER 17

Three months later
London, England

Noelle sat as still as she could. She was sharing a beautiful stone bench in the middle of Vauxhall Gardens with her new husband.

Benjamin lowered the arm he had curved protectively about her waist to just below her hip in order to give her derrière a surreptitious squeeze before returning to position.

Noelle tried her best not to squeeze him back.

The portrait artist poked his head out from behind the easel then returned his focus to his canvases.

He was making two records of this moment. A large likeness of Benjamin and Noelle for the hall of portraits in the primary Silkridge residence, and a miniature of Benjamin to fit the other half of the gold locket she wore next to her heart.

She risked a brief glance up at Benjamin from beneath her eyelashes.

He caught her in the act, and swooped in to steal a quick kiss.

"Not in front of the artist," she scolded him under her breath as her cheeks flushed with heat.

Benjamin's voice lowered huskily. "He's too busy working."

"What of the other people?" she reminded him, darting a glance over her shoulder at the hundreds of Londoners enjoying the beautiful weather and equally gorgeous flowers.

"Do face forward, Your Grace," Benjamin said with mock severity. "A professional artist is attempting to paint our portrait."

Noelle pinched his thigh. "Beast."

She had never been happier.

London was even larger than she had anticipated, and full of many more pleasures. She had made countless new friends, joined book clubs and charitable societies. And every moment that Parliament was not in session, Benjamin was by her side.

Last night, they had spent an exhilarating evening in his brand new opera box at the Royal Theatre. The night before, a soirée at the Ormondton residence. She and Benjamin had spent so much time waltzing in each other's arms these past few months, Noelle was once again in need of new dancing slippers.

The very best problem to have.

She received weekly reports from her apprentices in the counting house. The competent new team had the accounts well in hand. It felt like a miracle.

Noelle could *enjoy* her Season in London, and then enjoy the holiday season in Cressmouth. She leaned her head into Benjamin's shoulder and smiled contentedly. Where they were on the map didn't matter.

Anywhere they could be together was home.

The following December
Christmas, England

"I want a ride to the play!" called a lad bundled in so much winter clothing his face was barely visible.

With a practiced hand, Benjamin guided his sleigh to the side of the road. "Climb aboard. I believe there is an inch or two of room left."

His wife unsuccessfully stifled a giggle as the village children behind them jostled each other like a box of puppies to make room for the new arrival.

Although *The Winter's Tale* would not begin for another hour, this was their fifth trip through the village. Benjamin was starting to suspect that the children fled the amphitheater as soon as they arrived in order to sneak a sleigh ride again and again. Not that he minded.

Although his life was now split evenly between

two worlds, his heart belonged wholly with the woman at his side.

Some high-in-the-instep aristocrats looked down their snobbish noses at a duke making a love match, but Benjamin had no regrets whatsoever. Indeed, their united efforts toward making a difference in others' lives had made them something of a favorite in many circles.

Noelle had quickly become the perfect wife and partner. Over the past year, they shared intimate discussions about politics over matching cups of mint tea, and then spent blissful hours in the London whirl enjoying concerts and soirées and fireworks in the gardens. Her innate grace and sweetness had won plenty of new friends.

Life together in Cressmouth was just as delightful. He and Noelle had decided to build a private cottage rather than reside in the castle, and Benjamin could not be happier with that decision. He had come to love the sound of blustery winter wind outside while he and his wife heated up the evenings inside. He loved *Noelle*.

He lifted the brim of her bonnet to plant a quick kiss on one of her rosy cheeks.

"No kissing!" cried a chorus of young voices in the back from the sleigh.

A pelting of snowballs to the back of Benjamin's greatcoat immediately followed.

He scooped up whatever snow he could and tossed it back over his shoulder as he had done every other time he had temporarily "forgotten" the children's no kissing rule.

They screamed with delight as the loosely packed snow rained down on them in flutters of snowflakes.

"Here we are," Benjamin called out as he pulled the sleigh before the amphitheater. "Out you go. Find the best seats in the house!"

The children tumbled out of the sleigh and streamed toward the stage, but Benjamin had no doubt half a dozen would find their way back onto his path in the next quarter hour. Benjamin loved it. Moments like these were how holiday traditions were born.

"Happy Christmas to all!" Noelle laughingly called toward the children's retreating backs.

Benjamin nuzzled the curve of her neck. "And to us... a sizzling night."

His favorite tradition of all.

THE END

❧

What will happen when Penelope the no-non-sense perfumer sets her scientific sights on rakish scoundrel, "Saint Nick"?

Find out in *Kiss of a Duke*, the next romance in the *12 Dukes of Christmas* series!

Keep turning for a **Sneak Peek**!

❧

Want more Noelle & Benjamin?

Read a FREE second epilogue, exclusively for fans!

Grab your Love Letters here:
https://bookhip.com/XLPDWH

AUTHOR'S NOTE

"*H*umbug" has existed as a term since the 1700s, although it wasn't widely popularized until Charles Dickens' *A Christmas Carol* was published in 1843. His now-classic tale was unknown during the Regency period.

Perhaps because of this, it was so much fun to weave elements of homage into Benjamin and Noelle's romance. You may also spot nods to other holiday classics throughout the entire *12 Dukes of Christmas* series.

I hope you enjoy reading these stories as much as I've enjoyed writing them!

xoxo,

Erica

THANK YOU FOR READING

Love talking books with fellow readers?

Join the *Historical Romance Book Club* for prizes, books, and live chats with your favorite romance authors:
    Facebook.com/groups/HistRomBookClub

Check out the *12 Dukes of Christmas* facebook group for giveaways and exclusive content:
    Facebook.com/groups/DukesOfChristmas

Join the *Rogues to Riches* facebook group for insider info and first looks at future books in the series:
    Facebook.com/groups/RoguesToRiches

Check out the *Dukes of War* facebook group for giveaways and exclusive content:
    Facebook.com/groups/DukesOfWar

And check out the official website for sneak peeks and more:

www.EricaRidley.com/books

∼

Don't forget your free book!

Sign up at http://ridley.vip for members-only exclusives, including advance notice of pre-orders, as well as contests, giveaways, freebies, and 99¢ deals!

∼

KISS OF A DUKE

Just one more kiss... (Milady, it's cold outside)

Lady chemist Penelope Mitchell took England by storm with *Duke*, a perfume for men that has women swooning at their feet. To prove the same aphrodisiacal potency of her upcoming version for ladies, the new perfume must cause a rake to fall in love with her in ten days. And she has just the man in mind...

Sexy pleasure-seeker Nicholas Pringle—known as "Saint Nick" for his wicked ways—wants to end the absurd cologne that has every young buck believing himself a ladies' man. How hard can it be to charm a spinster into changing her mind? But when Penelope does the charming, this rakish scoundrel must decide between losing the war... or losing his heart.

SNEAK PEEK

Penelope wrenched out of Gloria's grasp and an-
gled her head toward the open ballroom doors.
"Where are they?"

Gloria fanned her throat. "Saint Nick is the
gentleman with—"

"Found him." The strangled words barely es-
caped Penelope's suddenly dry throat. Gloria was
right.

From a biological perspective, he was the finest
male specimen Penelope had ever seen. And as a
living, breathing woman... Good heavens.

Features: symmetrical. Jawline: chiseled. Vis-
age: arresting. Light brown hair tumbled over a
perfectly shaped head. His cravat was as white as
chemists' talcum, a subtle explosion of sharp
points and soft folds designed to add elegance
without distracting from the rest of the package.

And Saint Nick made one tempting package.

The hard curves of his muscled arms and wide
shoulders were shown to advantage in a dashing
coat of black superfine that begged to be touched.

His waistcoat was the shimmery silver of magnesium, an element oft-combined with iron. She wondered if his will was just as strong.

Coal-black boots, tight-fitting buckskins, kid gloves... All he'd need to do was jingle a bell and every woman present would clamor to be his.

Every woman but Penelope.

Yes, his looks were the very definition of all that was virile and desirable in a gentleman. But his approach to life made him the last man who could hold her interest. He was an accomplished rake. A man who relied on *romance* to woo silly women.

The urge to spread one's seed might be a natural male directive, but Penelope would never fawn over a man with nothing to recommend him beyond symmetrical features and pretty words. She had better things to do. Her mind preferred the comfort and excitement of her laboratory to pointless strolls down moonlit paths with a man who couldn't hold a meaningful conversation.

Penelope cared about facts, about science, about logic. A natural philosopher would never select a mating partner based on external beauty alone.

"Uninterested," she said abruptly. "Shall we find the dessert buffet?"

～

ACKNOWLEDGMENTS

As always, I could not have written this book without the invaluable support of my critique partners. Huge thanks go out to Erica Monroe and Morgan Edens. You are the best!

Lastly, I want to thank the *12 Dukes of Christmas* facebook group, my *Historical Romance Book Club,* and my fabulous street team. Your enthusiasm makes the romance happen.

Thank you so much!

ABOUT THE AUTHOR

Erica Ridley is a *New York Times* and *USA Today* best-selling author of historical romance novels.

In the new *12 Dukes of Christmas* series, enjoy witty, heartwarming Regency romps nestled in a picturesque snow-covered village. After all, nothing heats up a winter night quite like finding oneself in the arms of a duke!

Her two most popular series, the *Dukes of War* and *Rogues to Riches*, feature roguish peers and dashing war heroes who find love amongst the splendor and madness of Regency England.

When not reading or writing romances, Erica can be found riding camels in Africa, zip-lining through rainforests in Central America, or getting hopelessly lost in the middle of Budapest.

Let's be friends! Find Erica on:
www.EricaRidley.com

Made in the USA
Las Vegas, NV
11 December 2020

12573350R00125